ALL FOUR QUARTERS OF THE MOON

Also by Shirley Marr

Glasshouse of Stars

ALL FOUR QUARTERS OF THE MOON

SHIRLEY MARR

Simon & Schuster Books for Young Readers
NEW YORK   LONDON   TORONTO   SYDNEY   NEW DELHI

SIMON & SCHUSTER BOOKS FOR YOUNG READERS
An imprint of Simon & Schuster Children's Publishing Division
1230 Avenue of the Americas, New York, New York 10020
This book is a work of fiction. Any references to historical events, real people, or real places are used fictitiously. Other names, characters, places, and events are products of the author's imagination, and any resemblance to actual events or places or persons, living or dead, is entirely coincidental.
SIMON & SCHUSTER BOOKS FOR YOUNG READERS
and related marks are trademarks of Simon & Schuster, Inc.
For information about special discounts for bulk purchases, please contact Simon & Schuster Special Sales at 1-866-506-1949 or business@simonandschuster.com.
The Simon & Schuster Speakers Bureau can bring authors to your live event. For more information or to book an event, contact the Simon & Schuster Speakers Bureau at 1-866-248-3049 or visit our website at www.simonspeakers.com.
Interior design by Hilary Zarycky
The text for this book was set in Arrus.
Manufactured in the United States of America
0622 FFG
First Edition
2 4 6 8 10 9 7 5 3 1
Library of Congress Cataloging-in-Publication Data
Names: Marr, Shirley, author.
Title: All four quarters of the moon / Shirley Marr.
Description: First edition. | New York : Simon & Schuster Books for Young Readers, [2022] | Audience: Ages 8–12. | Audience: Grades 4–6. | Summary: Eleven-year-old Peijing and her family are adapting to their new life in Australia, but when cracks in her family life start to appear, she must find a way to cope with the uncertainties of her own little world and figure out where she fits in.
Identifiers: LCCN 2021055181 (print) | LCCN 2021055182 (ebook) | ISBN 9781534488861 (hardcover) | ISBN 9781534488885 (ebook)
Subjects: CYAC: Family life—Fiction. | Emigration and immigration—Fiction. | Chinese—Australia—Fiction. | Resilience (Personality trait)—Fiction. | Belonging (Social psychology)—Fiction. | LCGFT: Fiction.
Classification: LCC PZ7.1.M37265 Al 2022 (print) | LCC PZ7.1.M37265 (ebook) | DDC [Fic]—dc23
LC record available at https://lccn.loc.gov/2021055181
LC ebook record available at https://lccn.loc.gov/2021055182

ALL FOUR QUARTERS OF THE MOON

FIRST QUARTER
OF THE MOON

"Ah Ma told me that in the beginning there was nothing. Then there was an egg," said Biju dramatically. "A giant hatched out of the egg and started to push the heavens and the earth apart. That's how the universe was created."

"Is that so?" said Peijing, thinking carefully. "If there was nothing, then what created the egg?"

"Shhh," said Biju. "You're ruining the story. Anyway, that's not how the story really goes."

"Well, how, then?"

"In the beginning, there was an egg, and out of it hatched two sisters."

CHAPTER ONE

Ah Ma said she could tell if the mooncakes she was making that year for the Mid-Autumn Festival would be perfect or not just by the feel of the yolk. She had peeled the salted duck egg and weighed it with her hand. It was a good egg. She passed the golden middle to her granddaughter.

"Oh, no," said Peijing. Eager not to drop it into the sink, she had held on too tight. Now the yolk lay misshapen in her palm, no longer a miniature full moon.

Peijing looked out the kitchen window at the real full moon, hanging so yellow and round that it almost sat on top of all the apartment buildings surrounding their own. She felt as if the moon would drop out of the sky if she so much as breathed wrong.

The Guo family were very superstitious. There were things forbidden during the festival. Don't point at the moon or the goddess living there will cut your ear. Don't stare at the moon if you have recently given birth, gotten married, done a bad deal in business, or have too much yang energy in your body.

No one could ever explain properly to Peijing what this yang energy was.

"As the old proverb goes," replied Ah Ma, "there are no mistakes in life, only lessons." She smiled mysteriously and passed Peijing another egg yolk.

Ah Ma showed her how to wrap the washed yolks in lotus paste to make the mooncake filling. Peijing let out a breath she didn't even know she was holding. Ah Ma gently touched her on the shoulder, and she felt like they were sharing a secret.

The Guos were also a very traditional Chinese family who didn't believe in touching or hugging each other because it wasn't an honorable thing to hug or touch each other. But sometimes, as Peijing discovered, there were cracks in the rules for those who were very young and very old.

Out through the arched doorway that looked into the living room, where all of Peijing's aunts and uncles had come to play mahjong, she could hear the shrill voice of Second Aunty saying that she had to leave already. Second Aunty cleaned the airport for a living and had to wake up at five in the morning.

This was followed by the sound of crying. Peijing peered through the doorway, and there was Ma Ma with her face in her hands, looking vibrant in her new green housedress, but sounding as sad as a piece of tinkling jade.

It was definitely forbidden to cry during the Mid-Autumn Festival. Although Peijing was eleven years old now and considered herself far from being a child, she still didn't understand why adults would tell others not to do a thing and then do it themselves.

But it was no good—Second Aunty still had to wake up at five in the morning. Second Aunty told Ma Ma to stop crying. To think about how Ma Ma and her family were moving to Australia the next day. The move would improve Ma Ma's yin energy. It would be a lucky life. Not like Second Aunty, waking up at five in the morning, six days a week, to pick up disgusting things travelers left behind on airplanes. They didn't forget to take just their magazines, you know.

Peijing felt the nerves in her stomach. Block 222, Batu Bulan East Avenue 4, was the only home she had ever known.

She looked out the kitchen window to the playground. It was small and surrounded by the tall apartment blocks on all four sides, and kids would often fight to use the equipment, but Peijing liked how it felt contained and protected against the outside world. Safe. She could see her younger cousins strung out on the climbing frame, lighting up the night with sparklers like a constellation—even though they were definitely not allowed to play with matches. On the highest point of the frame, atop the rocket-ship slide, sat Peijing's little sister, five-year-old Biju, fearless against the dark.

"Come and help Ah Ma do the next step," said Ah Ma gently.

Peijing was sure "help" was too generous a word for her grandmother to use, as rolling out the sweet mooncake pastry was the hardest part. She was unsure if she could ever get it as thin as Ah Ma did without making a hole. She declined the rolling pin Ah Ma passed to her.

"How long have you been making mooncakes for?" asked Peijing, surprised that she had never thought to ask before.

"The womenfolk have always been making them as long as I know," replied Ah Ma. "My mother taught me, and her mother taught her. I can even remember my great-great-grandmother making them. It's the same family recipe."

Ah Ma leaned in closer to Peijing. "The secret lies in the homemade golden syrup."

Peijing marveled at Ah Ma's long memory. She felt a strange sensation about being the last on a long chain of these mooncake-making women, little Biju showing no interest in mooncakes other than eating them. Peijing felt anxious that she could only do the easy bits, as if time might just run out before she could learn to do it all.

That's if anyone made mooncakes in Australia anyway.

She had overheard conversations about how different things were going to be for Ba Ba, Ma Ma, Ah Ma, Biju, and her once they arrived. How they would have to learn new ways and new customs. How the stores there might not even sell salted duck eggs.

She wondered what they made for Mid-Autumn Festival in Australia. If they celebrated Mid-Autumn Festival at all.

Ah Ma pressed the pastry and the filling into the wooden molds, and Peijing watched as the mooncakes tumbled out, perfectly shaped and imprinted with mysterious designs on the top.

"What about these designs? What do they mean?" Peijing asked, tracing one of the mooncakes with her finger before hiding her hand behind her back.

"That, I don't know. These meanings have been lost in time. That symbol is so old that even someone as ancient as me can't understand it." Ah Ma chuckled and dabbed the pastry with an egg wash. "It is from before the first written language, when our ancestors used to pass stories from mouth to ear and try to hold them safe inside symbols. Stories would stay for eight thousand years, then stories would fade."

Peijing had been learning about the universe at school—the big bang, the first stars, the first single-celled life—and she knew, in the scheme of things, eight thousand years was just a blink of an eye. She was worried that this precise moment would disappear and would never come back again.

"But as the old saying goes," continued Ah Ma, "the palest ink is better than the best memory."

A written story could last forever. Peijing wasn't very good at writing her feelings down and she worried about that.

As the mooncakes baked away, Biju suddenly made her grand entrance into the kitchen, plum sauce from the duck she had eaten for mid-autumn dinner still around her mouth, her clothes smelling like firecrackers.

"I want one of those," she said loudly, peering through the glass into the oven.

She did not say "please." Manners were also very important to the Guos. As the eldest daughter, Peijing was a mirror, a reflection of her mother. So she was always careful about how she behaved. As her younger sister, Biju was a reflection of Peijing.

Well, supposed to be, anyway. Pejing pressed her lips together and sighed.

"Then you've arrived just in time." Ah Ma smiled. She didn't mention anything about Biju not saying "please." She pulled the hot rack out of the oven with a dishcloth.

Peijing looked at all the perfectly baked mooncakes in wonder, and she felt golden and magical. Biju placed her arms around Ah Ma and sank her face into Ah Ma's apron. Peijing wished she were still small enough to do the same.

"Let's see how they turned out." Ah Ma placed one on the cutting board and fetched a knife. Peijing found herself holding her breath again. As if her whole life depended on this moment. Ah Ma sliced down with the knife and pulled the two halves apart.

It was perfectly baked.

The yolk in the middle round and yellow.

Peijing let go and took a breath.

"Yuck!" yelled Biju. "I hate the ones with the stinky egg!"

As abruptly, the thin webbing that held the magic together, where the middle of a mooncake could be as big as the moon, was destroyed. Peijing knew Biju was only five and couldn't help it, but she wanted to remember this moment as perfect.

Ah Ma divided the mooncake into four pieces. Peijing picked up a slice and looked at the yolk, now a quarter moon, and felt haunted for reasons she could not explain. A cold, empty feeling like the vacuum of space. She popped the piece into her mouth. It tasted delicious. Salty, sweet, and crumbly.

"Don't worry. I'm going to make your favorite filling next. Sweet red bean with pumpkin seeds," Ah Ma said to Biju.

"Why didn't you make my favorite first?" Biju demanded and scrunched up her face. "I might be asleep by the time they finish cooking!"

Peijing sighed again. She always seemed to be sighing at one thing or another, carrying the weight of one responsibility or another on her shoulders. Biju, on the other hand, understood none of these things.

"My apologies. Ah Ma got it the wrong way around. Ah Ma is forgetful these days."

Biju suddenly went quiet.

"I was really looking forward to eating my last mooncake here," she said quietly and sucked on her fingers. "We don't know if anyone even makes moon-cakes in Australia."

And with that, it felt like the universe connected the two sisters again. Peijing's heart softened.

"Can I help with anything?" Ma Ma appeared in the kitchen, rubbing her face. Peijing did not want to tell her mother that one set of fake lashes on her perfectly made-up eyes was missing. Ma Ma was holding a mahjong tile in her hand. She deposited it absent-mindedly on top of the fridge.

Peijing stared up at the symbol for the East Wind.

Ah Ma set Ma Ma to work straightaway rolling pastry. While they were busy chatting, Peijing took her sister by the hand. Together they slipped away, past the adults playing mahjong, to their shared bed-room. Their bare feet moved faster as they approached the door.

To a world of their own.

"In the beginning, there was an egg, and out of it hatched two sisters," declared Biju. "They stood on either side and pushed up the sky together. So high up that heaven and earth would never meet again.

"Their imagination created all the animals, their tears created the rivers, the blackness of their hair the night sky, and the twinkle in their eyes all the stars. Oh, and the big sister's flaring temper created fire."

"Yes, that is true," said Peijing, "but you got the wrong sister."

"I don't think so!" replied Biju in a huff.

CHAPTER TWO

From under Biju's bed, a cardboard box was ceremoniously removed from its hiding place. It used to contain forty-eight packets of instant prawn noodles, the exclamation of HAR MEE HO LIAO! imprinted on the side. Now it held an entire world.

"At least in Australia we will still have the Little World," said Peijing.

"We might not make mooncakes anymore, but we will have the Little World," echoed Biju.

"Do you remember what I told you?" said Peijing solemnly.

Biju nodded.

"Tomorrow morning, we wake up early. We put all of the Little World into my suitcase."

Peijing knew it didn't matter if the Little World was placed into one or the other of the pull-along suitcases Ba Ba had bought for the two girls. But for some reason Peijing felt that, being the eldest, the honor needed to be hers. She thought about that new suitcase—supposedly tough enough to be thrown around in a plane, but startlingly fragile-looking in bird-egg blue—and she felt scared.

But the Little World was something familiar. Something safe. Something to escape into. Where minutes could become hours and hours grow into days. Where, in a blink of an eye, ecosystems could grow and flourish and collapse again back into the ocean, and large herds of beasts that only existed in your mind could cross from one continent to another. Where something you made yourself could be your home, even just for a while.

"Will the red barn go into the suitcase first?" asked Biju, her loud voice small now.

"Yes, of course it will," replied Peijing good-naturedly, even though she was annoyed at Biju for having to even ask the rules.

"Is everything going to fit?" Biju put her hand on top of the box and gave it a gentle push. The Little World had grown so vast it was threatening to spill out.

"It will fit," Peijing reassured her sister.

She had stuck to packing the bare essentials into that pull-along suitcase: an old special blanket and a new book on space. Sacrificed a pillow, a drawing kit, and a warm fuzzy pair of socks. Although she had never been on a plane before and these seemed like things she might possibly need, the Little World was more important.

"None of the animals will be hurt?"

"Of course not."

All the animals were made of paper, after all.

"Can I look at them one last time?"

Peijing rather preferred that the Little World stay exactly where it was. She had her superstitions too.

But the Little World was a shared world, so—very carefully, under her supervision—parts of it were allowed to be taken out and unfolded onto the floor. There were zoos and farms and a network of underground burrows and branches of trees made of many pieces of paper taped together.

There were oceans, rivers, and lakes, too, but, as some of them were so big they stretched from one side of the room to the other, they stayed in the box.

In the center of it was the red barn, with its great double door.

And all of it was populated by tiny individual animals that were carefully cut out, cherished, and placed into their homes. The Little World was a secret that not even Ma Ma or Ba Ba knew about.

It had started as a small act of defiance when Peijing would draw in the columns of her workbooks when she should be doing homework. Just things small enough to be hidden by the side of her hand if Ma Ma walked past. Later she took to cutting them out and hiding them in secret places.

Ma Ma seemed too busy to notice anyway. But Biju noticed. Maybe because she was small and therefore noticed incredibly small things that adults never did, like a ladybug sitting on the windowsill or a cicada resting on the old pedestal fan. Biju was allowed to join in once she proved she could use scissors properly, and also because it was nice to share sometimes, as keeping a secret is a lonely thing. The Little World was their own handmade heaven.

Peijing tried not to love it all too much. Otherwise she would start to suspect that she was good at drawing, and she really needed to be better at math and science because Ma Ma told her so.

She surveyed the land with a critical eye. There existed neat, meticulously drawn animals that reflected those on planet earth. Those were her creations. On the other hand, there were also strange, anatomically incorrect animals and animals that technically weren't necessarily even real animals that she had definitely played no part in. When Peijing thought about it, she and Biju couldn't be more different as two creators of the one world.

To fit in with the theme of the holiday, Biju had drawn a giant moon over four sheets of paper. It was wonky, and Peijing thought it looked more like a potato than a moon. Biju had also made the rabbit who lived there. Peijing thought the front paws were too big, the tail unrealistically drawn like a cotton ball instead of a prawn dumpling, but she didn't say anything because she was a good big sister.

Biju pressed her nose against the glass of their bedroom window and stared up at the mid-autumn moon.

"Look! See the real jade rabbit on the moon?"

Biju pointed to the marks that made up the ears, the feet, and the mortar and pestle the jade rabbit held between his paws. Pounding the elixir of immortality for the goddess who lived there all by herself.

Peijing knew the world couldn't exist without Biju's storytelling, but all she could say was, "Don't point at the moon! The goddess will cut your ear!"

Biju scowled. "I don't believe those dumb superstitions," she said, which Peijing thought was interesting since Biju believed there was a rabbit on the moon.

They were interrupted by a noise outside the

closed bedroom door, and the Little World was quickly packed away, the box pushed back into its hiding spot under the bed. Peijing straightened the blanket so it covered up the gap.

"Now I think it's time for you to go to bed," she told Biju.

"Are you going to bed too?" Biju answered back.

Peijing thought about it. She wanted to stay up for a little longer. "Not yet."

"That's unfair! Why do you get to stay up?" Biju stamped her feet.

"I'm older than you," replied Peijing, a perfectly reasonable explanation, she thought.

"I'm not tired," said Biju and yawned.

"Fine. Don't forget I'm just trying to be a good sister by reminding you we have a big journey ahead of us tomorrow," said Peijing. Her voice sounded sensible and responsible. She always sounded sensible and responsible.

She wondered if Biju, Ma Ma, Ba Ba, and even Ah Ma ever saw the real girl inside of her. The one with all the hairs on her body standing up like the scales of a scared pangolin. The one that longed to break free.

Biju ran out the door and didn't return even after Peijing called after her with a raised voice. Peijing shook her head and left the bedroom.

Out in the noise of the living room, her parents were engaged in a heated game, Ma Ma surveying her tiles with an inscrutable mahjong face, always the most competitive member of their family. Peijing thought about the East Wind tile still sitting on top of the fridge and wondered if its absence made a difference.

While the aunties and uncles talked about money and their aching joints, conversations regularly punctuated with a dismayed "Aiyah!," the cousins had come in from the playground and were sprawled on the couch watching TV and looking bored. Ah Ma was lying on the rattan armchair, legs splayed, eyes closed, and mouth open.

In the kitchen, Peijing found Biju in front of the red bean mooncakes now baking in the oven. The girl who claimed she was not tired was curled up on the tiles.

Peijing found herself shaking her head again. As gently as possible, she picked up her sister and half carried, half dragged her to the bathroom. There she brushed Biju's teeth for her, while Biju, tried to argue and fight.

She tucked Biju into bed, between the two large bolsters that made her sister feel safe. Biju fell asleep straightaway without a word of thanks.

Peijing sat down on her own bed and thought about the responsibilities that weighed were as heavy as the actual weight of her sister. It was her duty to look after Biju without question; her sensible mind knew that. But when she searched her heart, she knew she would do the same, even if she wasn't told to.

Biju was a reflection of her big sister, this was true, but Peijing could only hope she was as fierce and unafraid as her little sister. She laid her head on one of Biju's bolsters and felt hopeful for their future.

Although she said she was going to stay up later than her sister, she, too, fell asleep.

"Ah Ma told me how the jade rabbit got on the moon," said Biju.

"Will you promise not to point at the moon again?" said Peijing, and added cautiously from the side of her mouth, "You know what the goddess will—"

"No," said Biju.

Peijing sighed. "Tell me, then. How did the rabbit get on the moon?"

"He offered the most that anyone could ever offer," said Biju theatrically. "He made the biggest sacrifice anyone could ever make. So, in honor of this, the goddess took him to the moon with her, so everyone in the world can be reminded of this forevermore."

"Which is?"

"I'm not going to tell you because you're trying to get me in trouble with the goddess."

"Biju!"

CHAPTER THREE

Peijing and Biju woke up in the darkness the next morning to commence their secret plan. But Ma Ma was already up before them and came barging into the room without asking, giving orders and placing her hands on her hips. She was immaculately dressed in a white two-piece: a blouse and a pleated skirt with colored circles on it. Her permed hair was neatly styled. Peijing wondered how long Ma Ma had been up, but she didn't ask as it would be disrespectful.

Peijing looked at Biju, each of them on opposite sides of the kitchen table as they sat in their pajamas and ate coconut jam baos, hot out of the bamboo steamer. They both squirmed uncomfortably in their chairs, trying to act normal, waiting for a break so they could get to the Little World, which still sat inside its cardboard home under the bed.

Peijing was a little shy to even look at Ba Ba as she had rarely seen him out of his work clothes. Ba Ba usually worked all days of the week, even though he was supposed to have Sunday off. He looked unfamiliar in his polo shirt and casual pants.

Ma Ma tried to ask Ba Ba again if she could take the mahjong table along with them, as she had no idea if you could get one in Australia. But Ba Ba said no. It was too big. They would have all the new furniture they needed in the new house in Australia. Ba Ba's company was providing for all of that.

Anyway, they had already promised Second Uncle he could have the mahjong table. Ma Ma said fine, Second Uncle could have the mahjong table, then. But she still wrung her hands, touched the mahjong table one last time, and looked worried.

Peijing was busy noticing all the little details and trying to help Ah Ma, who had strangely forgotten to take the wrapper off the bottom of her bao and was trying to eat the whole thing, paper and all. Peijing didn't notice when Biju slipped away.

Until everyone heard the bloodcurdling scream from the bedroom.

Peijing looked at Ah Ma, then at Ma Ma and Ba Ba, before the four of them ran to the bedroom.

Biju was in there howling at the top of her lungs.

Ah Ma went inside first, as Ah Ma was the one with the magic touch when it came to the girls, but she came out after a while with a confused look on her face. There was nothing wrong with Biju. She just wouldn't stop screaming.

Ma Ma went next, and, since it was Biju's duty to listen to her mother, Biju's tantrum should have stopped. But the little girl opened up her mouth and another great howl came out. Ma Ma said she had no idea what was wrong. Biju wouldn't say.

Reluctantly, Ba Ba had a go. It wasn't his duty to get involved in the raising of the children, so all he had to say to Biju was that he was going to discipline her with the chicken feather duster if she didn't stop. This only caused her to howl even louder.

Peijing put her hands over her ears and went to stare at the kitchen clock. As much as she was nervous about leaving, at this rate they were all going to be late. They would miss their plane and they wouldn't be able to start their new life in Australia.

After the third hand on the clock traveled one whole circle, and Biju was still carrying on, Peijing went back into the bedroom, shooed everyone out, and closed the door.

"Are you going to tell me what the real matter is?" asked Peijing.

"I can't!" shouted Biju.

"Don't be silly, I'm your sister," said Peijing and sat down on the bed next to Biju.

A tear appeared on Biju's face, which she angrily brushed away. Silently, she got up off the bed and pulled the prawn noodle box out.

Peijing gasped.

She had been fully expecting this event.

She had been dreading it.

But even she had not expected it to happen on the very morning they were due to leave.

Whenever the box started to get too full, an event called an Extinction would occur. Sometimes up to half the world would suddenly disappear. One time— during the very worst of the Great Extinctions—only the red barn was left at the bottom, seemingly having escaped for no explainable reason.

Of course, Peijing knew it was Ma Ma who was responsible for the Extinctions. The last one correlated with the time six months ago when Ba Ba told Ma Ma he was taking the job at the new office in Australia. But Peijing felt the need to lie and shelter Biju from this fact, concocting an elaborate story about how, like the real world, the Little World also suffered from catastrophic events. The greenhouse effect, tectonic shifts, melting ice caps.

Biju would make faces and yell at the heavens, balling her hands into fists and being dramatic in the way all the Guo women were dramatic, but she accepted it. Sometimes Peijing worried about what would happen if Biju found out the truth. She wondered if her sister already knew and just didn't want to face it.

But this Extinction was worse.

There was nothing left in the box.

Never since its existence had the Little World suffered a complete Extinction such as this.

"Do you remember the dinosaurs?" said Peijing, grabbing Biju's arm. "The falling meteorite? The way the little mammals hid away safely and emerged after the dust settled and the sun came back out? I need you to focus on that."

Peijing ran her hand desperately all along the sides and bottom of the box as it taunted her, HAR MEE HO LIAO!

Finally, from under a flap, she drew out a single scrap of paper. It was the crushed jade rabbit, concertinaed together so that his head came comically straight out of his hind end, a very sad rabbit.

"This is enough," said Peijing, pressing it into Biju's hand. "To restart the whole world. Now listen carefully. Take the rabbit and hide him in your suitcase. It is your great responsibility not to lose him, okay?"

Biju nodded.

The vision inside of Peijing's head, the one where she carried the whole of the Little World to the new world, like so many mass migrations and geographical shifts in history before, vanished without a trace. A feeling of resentment against Ma Ma traveled into her heart.

But, just as quickly, Peijing pushed the thought out. Ma Ma always told her she had to be a good girl because all her ancestors could see her, like when she'd read how Santa Claus could see all the Western kids being either naughty or nice. Just without any sort of present at the end as a reward for behaving.

"When we reach the other side, the first thing that must be rebuilt is the red barn. Then the rest will follow, do you understand?"

Biju nodded again. She wasn't screaming anymore.

"Am I really allowed to be the one to carry him?" she asked.

"You drew him, so yes."

Biju folded her fingers carefully over the paper rabbit. The girls stood staring at Biju's closed hand. Peijing had the dreaded thought that if Biju opened it at the wrong time the rabbit would disappear, like an awful magic trick.

She didn't know why Biju was standing there so silently, though.

Yes, she did. Biju had that look on her face that said she still had another secret trying to burst out.

"You were right!" Biju exclaimed.

"What are you talking about?" replied Peijing. "I'm never right."

"I pointed at the mid-autumn moon, and the goddess cut my ear!"

Biju turned to the side and revealed the skin behind her right ear. Peijing squinted at it. At a stretch, it could be a celestial cut, but it looked more like a scratch that Biju probably made while she was sleeping.

Peijing was going to point this out, but the look on Biju's face suggested she might start screaming again.

"This is what you need to do," said Peijing, putting on her most practical voice. "Tonight, you will say sorry to the goddess in the moon." Peijing clasped her hands together in prayer and shook them up and down. "Then the scratch will disappear."

"Are you sure?"

"I promise, Mei Mei. Remember last weekend

when we were at the temple? While you were busy trying to prank me by hiding my flip-flops in the sea of shoes outside? I saw someone with this exact problem ask the question, and that was the answer the Tao master gave."

Biju stopped grimacing, and a small smile appeared on her face. Unexpectedly, she threw her arms around Peijing's waist and squeezed her tight.

"Thank you, Jie Jie! You always know how to fix things."

Peijing hoped in her heart of hearts that this would always be true.

She wasn't going to tell Biju that she had just made the whole thing up.

Yes, she had been observant inside the temple that day. She had been busy shaking fortune sticks and trying to look serious and grave, when in fact she was simply asking the oracle the chances of chicken rice for dinner.

Peijing took out a little plastic container from her travel bag, a gift of magical cure-all from an aunt who had been to Australia on a holiday. VASELINE: WHITE PETROLEUM JELLY, read the white letters on the blue sticker. Peijing scooped out some of the sticky substance and rubbed it on Biju's scratch. Biju complained it stung, even though Peijing knew the cure-all was soothing and would heal up the scratch with any luck by tomorrow.

She smoothed out Biju's damp bangs on the pretense that she was just straightening it. Then they parted—Biju to hide the rabbit and Peijing to struggle with where to put all her big feelings—before they came back together to stare down at their respective beds.

Placed there by Ma Ma were the expensive outfits that always came out for special occasions. Two identical sky-blue party dresses made from a stiff, rustling fabric. Peijing was eleven and not five like her little sister, but it didn't occur to her to be embarrassed. After all, when she went to birthday parties with girls the same age as her, they all wore the same types of dresses.

The embarrassment would come later, in Australia.

"What's wrong with Biju?" asked Ma Ma with a frown on her face as the sisters came out of the bedroom.

"Growing pains," replied Peijing and dodged any more questions.

With Biju's drama out of the way, the family packed up their suitcases and left their apartment for good. While in the taxi, Biju insisted on having her suitcase at her feet, and she kept one hand on it the entire trip. She secretly said that she could feel the cut on her ear healing already. Peijing smiled to herself.

They got to the airport on time.

"Ah Ma also told me about how the goddess came to be on the moon in the first place," said Biju.

"On a rocket ship, right?" said Peijing.

"Don't be silly," said Biju, "These tales are thousands of years old and they didn't have rocket ships back then."

"I guess that makes sense," said Peijing. It did not make any sense to her.

"Back in ancient times, there used to be ten crows who could turn into ten suns. These suns all took turns to rise in the sky. Until one day, they all rose into the sky at the same time."

"Oh, that sounds like it could be as hot as Australia," said Peijing.

She couldn't imagine it. All she had known was the humidity of Singapore: stepping out of the shower and the water droplets on her body turning into sweat before she had a chance to dry off.

"So that meant all the crops failed, all the rivers dried up, and the animals started to die," said Biju. "Everyone cried and cried, but it was so hot no tears came out."

CHAPTER FOUR

Biju had always referred to her older sister by the title Jie Jie. Peijing referred to Biju as Mei Mei. The prospect of anything else would be as horrifying as calling Ma Ma and Ba Ba and Ah Ma by their real names.

But while waiting for the boarding lounge to open at the airport, Biju made herself a friend of the same age and started a boisterous game of chasey, even though the two were told by both sets of families to stop running around and to sit down. Biju's new friend did not call either her older sister or brother by any formal titles. She called them Zoe and Ben.

Peijing looked at all the magazines and sweets in the newsstand trying to distract herself, but she still felt nervous, her belly heavy. She couldn't think of anything worse than making friends with someone who was catching a completely different plane to a completely different country, and the awful good-bye that would come with never seeing that person ever again. But she kept her feelings to herself, where they multiplied in the pit of her stomach like snakes.

Biju ran up to her sister and, with a cheeky grin, called her Peijing.

Peijing was a little taken aback, but a smile broke out on her face, and she called her sister Biju.

Maybe when they arrived in Australia, they could just use their real names with each other. Lately, Biju had been at times calling her Chair Chair instead of Jie Jie and had started shortening it to just Chair. Honestly, she would prefer being called Peijing.

Biju brought her new friend over for an introduction.

"Hello, Peijing," the new friend said.

Peijing found that she did not mind the friend not calling her Jie Jie, even though it was expected of anyone younger than her to use the title as well.

"Hello, Hualing," the new friend said to Ma Ma.

Ma Ma, on the other hand, minded dreadfully that the friend did not call her Aunty. Everyone who was younger than her was supposed to call her Aunty regardless of whether they were related to her or not.

"How did this friend even know my first name, anyway?" Ma Ma complained to Ba Ba. When Biju was told that she was going to be disciplined, she burst into tears.

"It's not my fault! It's just so confusing!" Biju exclaimed as she followed the rest of them into the boarding lounge that had now opened, sinking dejectedly into a chair. "I wish everyone went by their real names!"

"You can call me Peijing," she whispered, and took the blanket out of her suitcase and tucked it around Biju's shoulders.

That thing that Ma Ma had said about learning new ways to do things in the new country—maybe that started right now. She thought about the falling meteorite of the last great extinction on earth. How the animals hidden in the trees had to learn to come down again. How the dinosaurs that did survive took to the air and became birds.

"Maybe we can use each other's names in secret," she added as a precaution. She looked over to Ma Ma, but then smiled at Biju. "Another secret. Like the Little World."

This made Biju light up, as she did very much like secrets too.

Meanwhile, the new friend and her family had left to continue on the next stage of their journey. It appeared that Biju had suddenly forgotten all about them. Peijing wished things were that easy for her.

A voice came on over the intercom. Peijing's stomach sank again. They passed through the gate, which was scary because Peijing was sure somehow all their documents would be wrong. They walked down the long tunnel toward the entrance of the plane, which made her feel like there was definitely no going back. The acrid smell of the onboard air hit her like a force.

Peijing had never felt a love for her sister as large as she did in that moment. She feared for what her sister could not fear yet. She worried that she wasn't grateful enough for the opportunity Ba Ba was providing the family. She worried that she was too young to support Ma Ma much. She worried Biju was too little for all of this. Ah Ma maybe too old.

She searched for a way to protect Biju, because there were so many things they had yet to experience that were unknown, dangerous even—the food, the traditions, the customs, the clothing, and, of course, the famous poisonous snakes of Australia.

But Biju's only worry was what in-flight movie was going to play. The feelings inside of Peijing snaked faster. She let Biju have the window seat.

Ma Ma checked that both sisters were belted in, along with Ah Ma, who sat closest to the aisle. Peijing felt a little reassured by the act, but not enough.

She put one fearful hand on her grandmother.

"Don't worry about us," replied her grandmother, patting her on the shoulder.

"Huh?" said Peijing.

"I know you are worrying about everyone else, but don't forget you are also making a sacrifice. Like the rabbit in the moon," added Ah Ma mysteriously.

"Oh," said Peijing.

"You're a good, caring girl. Candy?"

Ah Ma revealed a packet of sweets, all different colors individually wrapped in clear cellophane. Peijing selected a pink one, twisted it open, and popped it into her mouth. It was strawberry-flavored, just as she had expected, and she felt reassured.

"You can always talk to your Ah Ma. Remember that."

Peijing touched her stomach. Just having Ah Ma say that meant the snakes had settled.

The plane took off, and it was the scariest thing ever. Peijing felt herself being pulled back, as if her entire being were pressing down on her, and she was aware of music being played in the background, like a soundtrack to her life she couldn't quite hear.

But then everything righted itself and the sign for seat belts turned off. The big screen at the front played a sad film about a struggling family, but one with a happy ending where everyone agreed to get along. Lunch was served, and, although the strange compressed air around her seemed to compress her appetite as well, Peijing was glad to see the food in front of her separated neatly into its various compartments, everything in its rightful place.

"Thanks, Ah Ma," whispered Peijing after the longest while.

Ah Ma just smiled knowingly.

Time passed. Long and short at the same time. Peijing simultaneously bored and overwhelmed. Suddenly, the captain announced the plane was descending, the seat belt sign came back on, and the snaking feeling inside of Peijing came back. Biju excitedly told her sister to look out the porthole, and they saw a land that was so . . . brown. *Where are all the people?* thought Peijing, but Biju grabbed her arm and pointed to a field of little sheep and little cows.

"Just like the Little World," she said.

Peijing placed her hand affectionately on one of Biju's plaits, and her sister turned to her questioningly.

"Nothing," said Peijing, even though it was everything.

She swallowed her nervousness and tried to climb away into little secret worlds.

"Proceeding to land," said the captain.

"Look," whispered Biju. She pressed the paper rabbit against the glass of the porthole. Although she had smoothed it over and over gently, it was still crumpled. The rabbit shone against the bright early morning sky. The moon was long gone.

"Put that away!" hissed Peijing. Although half-terrified that Biju was going to lose it, she was glad to see that rabbit. It was all they had left of the old world, until they began again.

"Naughty goddess cut Biju's ear! See you later, says the jade rabbit! Oh, no! Who is going to make the immortality elixir for the goddess now? She will have to become mortal and die!" Biju exclaimed, and made a whooshing noise as she slid the rabbit down the glass, dropping it out of the sky.

The rough feel of the tarmac under the plane's wheels came too suddenly and jolted Peijing back into her seat. The plane did a slow loop on the runway, and Peijing felt her stomach do the same. Then everything stopped. Peijing held on to that moment, wanted it to stay that way. But then everything started up really fast, with people standing up and removing their luggage from the overhead compartments and trying to push themselves down the aisle.

The flight attendant said, "See you later," and

Peijing thought this was a funny thing to say when she would likely never see these people again. Her head spun with images of rabbits, a lonely moon goddess and home. She looked out at the long stretch of tarmac in front of them. She put her foot on the top of the stairs.

Beside her came a sigh, and Ah Ma whispered, almost as if to herself, "The mid-autumn moon is the brightest; with every festival the homesickness multiples."

Peijing took one step down the clunky metal stairs and started her journey.

Different countries, like different people, had different scents. Singapore smelled sweet and humid and slightly rotten, like overripe tropical fruit. Australia smelled dry and dusty and a bit burnt, like something had been on fire for a very long time. Peijing immediately missed her home. She wondered if she was the only one noticing this, or if she just thought too much, felt too strongly.

The Guo family collected their suitcases at the baggage carousel, got checked by customs that they were not bringing into the country things that were considered too strange and wonderful, and were told they could proceed.

Through the exit they wheeled, past people who were waiting to glimpse their loved ones and looking disappointed to see the Guos instead, until they reached the front of the airport. Through the whooshing automatic doors they stepped out, into this strange, hot world.

It was, impossibly, hotter than anything Peijing could ever have imagined.

"With the ten suns in the sky all at once, it got so hot that the people begged the king to do something about it," said Biju. "The king agreed because, even though he lived in a huge stone palace, he was starting to feel the heat too."

"They didn't have air-conditioning in those days," said Peijing wisely.

"The king hired this famous archer. He had a good history of taking care of unruly beasts. Once, he defeated a monster with a body of a tiger and a head of a dragon that wailed like a baby. Another time, he defeated one that had the body of a giant serpent and nine crying baby heads. Don't get me started on the one that could swallow elephants whole and that also cried like a baby."

"Babies really are the scariest things," said Peijing, who, being the eldest child of the extended Guo family tree, had seen her fair share of screaming infant cousins.

"The archer tried to reason with the ten suns, but they refused to listen."

CHAPTER FIVE

Some things remained the same. Ba Ba went to work and wore the same easy-care polyester suit and tie and carried the same brown briefcase. Ma Ma stayed at home and cooked and cleaned and at the end of the day became so tired she had to go lie down, even though the change was supposed to help her yin energy. Ah Ma answered all of Peijing's and Biju's questions, as she was the wisest person they knew, and played with them when Ma Ma went to have her lie-down.

Some things were a little different, like how Ba Ba now worked five days a week instead of almost always seven. And he came home at five o'clock instead of coming home on some days after everyone had gone to bed. But when he was home, the plans he had of spending more time with his family consisted mostly of going into his study and shutting the door.

Some things were very different, like the house they were living in. The five of them no longer had to share a small apartment in Batu Bulan and instead lived in a whole house on Blueberry Street. Ma Ma was hesitant to go inside.

"Come and see our beautiful new place," said Ba Ba when they first arrived, but Ma Ma shook her head and pointed at the letter box.

Number 4.

Ma Ma was sure it was a sign of bad luck ahead.

Once they convinced Ma Ma to come in, they found that 4 Blueberry Street was indeed beautiful, with brand-new pink carpet and pale pink walls, as was the latest fashion. The pink wall tiles in the bathroom shone like little squares of candy. "Don't lick them," Peijing warned Biju. Biju just pretended.

In the bedroom at the back of the house, Peijing found a white wooden dressing table with a frilled skirt, like something from her wildest dreams. The dressing table itself was almost as big as her old room. On the bedside table there was a pink princess phone, unconnected to the wall.

Peijing had never known such space. Sometimes she even felt too scared to move. Like everything that had previously protected her had been pulled back and she was now exposed. She was silently grateful when Biju said she still wanted to share a bedroom. She wasn't ready to be alone yet.

The people and the atmosphere and the trees and the space were also different. From the living room window, Peijing could see the park across the road, and it was the biggest, greenest, flattest thing she had ever seen. Against the cloudless blue sky, the people walking their dogs looked like tiny specks. The horizon was huge, and when she stared at it for too long she felt dizzy.

Peijing believed she could take all the tall buildings and apartment blocks and skyscrapers from Singapore and drop them on that park, and this strange new sky would still be the biggest thing.

Some things were sort of the same, but with a twist. Like the supermarkets, which more or less looked much the same everywhere except, wandering the aisles, Peijing would suddenly come across a section that she had never seen before. Like the one for breakfast foods.

Peijing had never known that a complete breakfast could be contained in one neat rectangular cardboard box, some of them even offering prizes. The most thrilling, though, was the snacks and candy section, which shone colorful, plastic, and alien.

She looked for mooncakes at the supermarket,

as there would still be lots of store-made mooncakes after Mid-Autumn Festival, usually on special by now, but there were none.

Peijing didn't want to tell Ah Ma this, as it might upset her. In fact, she didn't know how Ah Ma felt at all. Their grandmother used to do tai chi in the park and play checkers at the communal tables at the bottom of their Singapore apartment block with the other elderly folk, but now she just stayed inside. The only time she went outside was to go sit in the backyard and stare at the lawn that was so newly rolled out you could still see the joins.

On a Sunday morning, a week after they had moved in, when Ma Ma once again said she wasn't ready to leave the house yet, Peijing became unexpectedly cross and bold. But then again, she wasn't sure if she was acting out of character because she wasn't sure what character she had become. She made Ba Ba leave his study and take everyone else out, even Ah Ma. Ba Ba seemed as lost as Ma Ma did in Australia. He didn't know where to take them, so he took them to the corner store.

Ba Ba bought Peijing a bag of cheese-flavored rings that looked like the ones she had known back home. But when she popped one in her mouth, they tasted wrong. Salty instead of sweet. Peijing stared at her fingers, stained orange, and was suddenly hit with a wave of homesickness, but she didn't say anything. This was her home now. She searched the sky for an outline of the moon, but it was way too early.

Biju showed Peijing the giant candy snake she had chosen, glowing with all colors of the rainbow.

"I will let you have half," said Biju very seriously to her sister. "But I am going to have the end with the head."

Ah Ma happily ate a green-colored ice cream and said it was the best pistachio she had ever tasted, even though it was mint.

Some things were still secret, like the Little World. The resurrection of the red barn was now complete, and the farm animals had come back. Soon all the forests would be back too. Peijing had asked Ba Ba for a box and had received one with the mysterious inscription 24 X 200G ARNOTT'S TIM TAMS on the side. It was not quite the same as the prawn noodle box, but like all other things was a sacrifice and a new beginning. From time to time Peijing still thought about the box tucked underneath her old bed. Empty and extinct.

The Little World flourished. Biju had started making kangaroos, koalas, and wombats because they were in Australia now. Biju said that everything in Australia had a pouch because that meant that mothers did not have to leave their babies behind. It was a fashion that started with the wallabies, she believed, but before you knew it, every animal had gotten herself a pouch.

After they returned from the corner store, Ma Ma said they had exactly one hour in their room before dinner. The Arnott's Tim Tams box was ceremoniously placed in the middle of the floor, sheets of white paper and tins of colored pencils hastily grabbed from drawers and spread out. The best pair of scissors passed from one eager set of hands to the other.

A new moon had been created, this time by Peijing, who made sure it was perfectly accurate. No rabbit- or goddess-shaped shadows on the surface, just dried seabeds, mountains, and craters. Unfortunate pockmarks. But she was still critical of the way it looked.

Peijing wanted the moon she drew to be as perfect as the one inside the fantasy that lodged itself in the deepest and most secret place in her heart. She imagined it displayed upon a gray felt board in a white room and, standing in front of it, judges with serious faces ticking boxes upon clipboards. In this dream, the judges nodded their heads at one another and then asked to shake her hand, as they revealed that she, Peijing Guo, was successful in gaining entry to a prestigious art school. Far, far away.

But Ma Ma thought growing up to be an artist was a bad thing, as all artists were starving artists for a reason. Ma Ma did not want Peijing to be poor, even if that meant she couldn't do what she loved when she was an adult. Ma Ma said she knew what poverty was, and it wasn't for Peijing.

Sensibly, at the back of her mind, Peijing knew if she told herself she wasn't good at drawing she would be happier to end up as something else—an engineer, an accountant, or a postdoctorate astrophysics researcher—and it would be for the best.

The new moon was created, but the rabbit did not go back. Biju hid him in the woods. The rabbit was still hiding from the goddess, she explained. The goddess was getting a little desperate for the immortality elixir now; overnight her beautiful young face had collapsed. Although the cut behind Biju's ear had already physically healed, some trace of it still remained in her mind.

Peijing stared at her sister in wonder. At the way Biju took old stories that Ah Ma and Ma Ma had told her and added her own strange and curious twists until they became the story of the two sisters.

It was a peculiar feeling to acknowledge that Biju was the storyteller and Peijing was the artist, that they were two similar but different stars dancing around each other, occasionally touching orbits. It was comforting; having Biju there meant Peijing wasn't alone, that Biju would perhaps one day tell the sisters' stories to their own children, just like a folktale. Perhaps, once they were down in ink, their stories would live longer than eight thousand years, could live forever.

But Biju was only five and couldn't quite write, and Peijing feared that things would be lost in the meantime.

They found Ma Ma on the phone when they went back out into the kitchen. She had stretched the long cord attached to the receiver all the way to her bedroom at the front, and her words were muffled, but her crying was very clear.

Peijing went hot in the face and tried to cover it up, even though she didn't know who their mother was talking to and why. She steered Biju to the living room, where Ah Ma was sitting watching the TV, like she did most of the time these days without their many aunts, uncles, and cousins to entertain her.

Peijing found out later who she was talking to

when Ba Ba asked Ma Ma about the huge bill that had been racked up in overseas calls back to Singapore. Ma Ma cried again and said she didn't like being so far away from her sisters, and that she felt lost and without a purpose.

Peijing couldn't protect Biju from adult feelings then.

"What is wrong with Ma Ma?" wailed Biju.

"It's just taking Ma Ma time to adjust to living here," replied Peijing.

"Well, I feel fine," said Biju.

"Adults have bigger bodies," said Peijing, thinking carefully about it. "Therefore, they are filled with more emotions. So it takes them longer than kids."

Later that night, the two sisters went outside to lie on the lawn and gaze up at the stars. Peijing was unafraid of the sky at night when it wore a black veil. Without the lights of all the flats and skyscrapers back at their old home, more stars revealed themselves in the darkness. It was all so beautiful it made Peijing's eyes ache.

The moon had become round and full again, but it was not the same mid-autumn moon. Peijing understood that the shadows on the surface were just geography—dried seabeds, mountains, craters, and unfortunate pockmarks—but found herself thinking instead of stories. Wondering if the rabbit had gone back home and all was well with the goddess again, or if the rabbit was still somewhere in the woods. Peijing's mind stretched with thoughts that had never been there before.

Biju pointed out constellations—an ox, a girl, a ghost, a hairy head, and an emptiness.

Peijing asked why there was a star map for "emptiness" but received no reply. When she propped herself up on her elbow, she found Biju had fallen asleep, the little girl tuckered out after a long day. Peijing lay back and closed her eyes as well, looking inside of herself to find her dreams.

"The ten suns refused to move no matter what the archer tried to do to get them to move," said Biju. "Then they decided to go in different directions. Can you imagine how hard it is to herd ten suns?"

"It is probably as hard as herding cats," Peijing said in all seriousness.

"He did end up herding them from one end of the sky to the other," said Biju, "but that just set the whole land on fire."

CHAPTER SIX

Two sets of school uniforms appeared mysteriously in the living room one day, and Peijing felt the funny gut feeling from the plane hit with the same hardness. That acrid smell. That twisting feeling. Except this time, it affected her heart as well. She suddenly thought of her best friends, Mei and Yifen, back in Singapore, carrying on their lives without her. Giggling in the back seat of the school bus. Going to the public pool on the weekend. Taking funny snaps in the photo booth at the shopping center, pulling faces.

Peijing picked up the yellow polo shirt and the pleated navy-blue skirt. Touched the embroidered patch with the school logo and then placed it all back down again. She expected Biju, standing next to her, to be as unfussed as she was about everything else, letting life slide down her back like water off a mandarin duck. But for the first time, she felt her sister tense up too.

Biju, with her arms linked behind her back, lowered her face and looked at her new school uniform with the unimpressed expression of a little old lady looking at a less-than-fresh piece of fish at the morning market. Then, without a sound, she took off.

Ma Ma crossed her arms and sighed.

"I would have been so grateful as a girl to come to another country and go to an English-speaking school," said Ma Ma, even though she had been in Australia for a month now and hadn't left the house.

Peijing did what she usually did. She counted silently to five in her head, her lucky number, and then she crept away to find her sister. She found Biju in their shared bedroom, hidden underneath her two giant bolster pillows.

"What's wrong?" asked Peijing.

"I never said that there was anything wrong," came the muffled reply.

"I can just tell. That's all." Peijing put her palm against her tummy and touched her own nervousness there. Snakes.

"I don't want to go to school. I just want to stay at home with Ah Ma and make things for the Little World," said Biju, revealing her face.

"I know you are unsure because it's your first time going to school."

No comment from Biju.

Peijing continued. "But we are going to the same school. We'll just be in different classes, that's all. I'll always be close by. And you will like school. I like school."

It was true. Peijing did like school. She missed Mei and Yifen and how they used to eat together with their matching lunch boxes and afterward play four square. Her old uniform, a pale blue pinafore with a white blouse. And as much as she didn't like to think it true, she even missed her strict teacher, Sister Lee.

Peijing missed belonging to something. She envied that Biju got to start at the beginning, not knowing anything else. Peijing knew exactly what she had left behind, and when she started school here, she probably wouldn't be able to keep herself from comparing everything.

Biju's face came out from underneath the pillows along with the rest of her.

"I'll be a big girl like you, going to school," she said thoughtfully.

"Well, you don't want anyone thinking you're a baby," said Peijing.

"I'm not a baby," said Biju, and she popped up and bounced out of the bedroom.

When Peijing eventually got up herself, she found her sister back out in the living room, having put on her new school uniform. She was in the midst of spinning around in a circle for Ma Ma and Ah Ma to see. Peijing secretly smiled.

The following Saturday morning, Ma Ma said she was ready to go out. She had to be, because she was going to be the one to pick up the girls after school, once they started going. Ma Ma put on her pink two-piece outfit, the one with the pleated skirt and the blouse with the shoulder pads. Before they left Singapore, she had bought five new two-piece sets and three new print dresses from OG, probably because she thought you couldn't get clothes in Australia, Peijing wasn't sure. Ma Ma put a pink color on her lips and cheeks.

Ma Ma knocked on the study door and told Ba Ba to make sure he came out once in a while to check on Ah Ma. Ba Ba didn't reply.

The three of them walked across that big park. Biju was still in her new school uniform even though it was the weekend. She was still spinning.

Although Peijing had looked out at that endless green every day from the window in the front room, she was not prepared for the experience. Peijing felt her knees buckle under the tremendousness of the blue sky. A great pattern of clouds had formed, slashed in half on the diagonal by some invisible force. Peijing believed if she started walking, she wouldn't get any-where because she had gotten so small.

Ma Ma pointed to the new school that the girls would be attending. Biju wanted to know which classroom was hers. Ma Ma did not know. Peijing concentrated on missing the cracks in the pavement and dared not look up.

They went next door to the school supplies store. Ma Ma scanned the list of things that Peijing needed to take on the first day of school, even though she could not read it herself. Peijing could read most of it, although she had no idea what on earth a "jotter" could be.

She grabbed hold of Biju, who wanted to beeline over to the pens display and start trying each one out. Peijing found herself distracted too, by a poster on the pinup board that read, LOOK BEFORE YOU DIVE—A SCHOOL POSTER COMPETITION BY THE SUMMERLAKE SURF LIFESAVING CLUB. CERTIFICATES AND PRIZES TO BE WON! But she kept her sensible head and quietly pocketed a leaflet, staying close to Ma Ma.

"Do you think we just pick from the shelves what

we need?" Ma Ma whispered. Peijing didn't know why Ma Ma was whispering, it wasn't like they were in a library. "Or do we show the list to someone and they pack it for us?"

Peijing shrugged. Ma Ma decided that Peijing should ask the person at the counter, so they all stood at the start of the line and waited for the person to call them. Ma Ma smoothed down the front of her pleated skirt. To their surprise, the lady there ignored them. Ma Ma waved to her, but she did not wave back. In fact, it looked like she was purposely trying not to see them.

Ma Ma frowned and crossed her arms. Peijing looked down at herself to see if the sky from the park had rubbed off and she had accidentally become invisible.

A man with a basket of stationery approached from behind, and Peijing was glad. If a line was forming, then the lady would have to start serving people.

"You can come right up, Mr. Moss," said the lady brightly.

"Excuse me."

The man with the stationery walked around them and went right up to the counter. The lady smiled, made small conversation, and started ringing his things up on the cash register. Ma Ma looked even angrier. Peijing scanned the store and felt hopeless. Not knowing what else to do, they just stood there.

The man finished being served and took his paper bag with his things inside and left the store. The lady went back to staring straight ahead of her. Peijing felt her arm being tugged forward, and she was jerked right up to the front counter by Ma Ma, who slammed the school list down.

The lady finally had to look at Ma Ma.

She looked at Ma Ma for a long time.

Then she pointed to the sign above the line. Peijing, with her face bright red, was forced to translate it: TEACHERS ONLY.

The lady pointed to the line beside it: GENERAL PUBLIC.

But there was nobody serving at that counter.

The lady did not go behind that counter to serve them. Peijing only realized she didn't want to serve them at all when she went away to another part of the store and started straightening the shelves.

Peijing looked at Ma Ma, then Biju, then stared down at herself and wondered what was wrong with them.

Ma Ma picked up the list, shoved it back into her handbag, then took Peijing and Biju by the hand and dragged them from the store. Biju protested because she wanted to look at the pens; there were some glitter ones. Peijing dared not look at Ma Ma's face in case her mother started crying, and the thought of that was mortifying.

Ba Ba was still in the study when they got back, and Peijing wondered if he had come out at all to check on Ah Ma like he was told to. Ma Ma went into the bedroom and slammed the door. Peijing and Biju checked on Ah Ma and found her asleep in her bedroom. Left by themselves, they climbed into their own secret world too. One made of paper, colored with love and held together with only tape.

That night, Ma Ma told Ba Ba that he had to go to the supplies store himself and get the things Peijing needed for school. She didn't explain why they had not bought them today. All Peijing knew was that the following day, a large brown paper bag mysteriously appeared on her bed, with all the stationery on the list.

A jotter disappointingly turned out to be just a plain pad of paper. No one ever talked about this incident again. A little while afterward, Ma Ma stopped wearing her nice two-piece outfits and print dresses as she said she had nowhere to go in them, no friends to visit. She said none of the stores were welcoming, even though Peijing thought they looked very welcoming, with many things to buy that had not been available in Singapore.

Ma Ma started wearing old T-shirts and jeans instead and didn't venture outside their house walls except to reluctantly do the food shopping. She became quick of temper and opinion, her daughters scattering to get out from underneath her feet.

"So, in desperation, the archer started to shoot the suns out of the sky with his bow and arrow. As each sun fell out of the sky, it turned back into a three-legged crow."

"A three-legged crow would be much sturdier than a two-legged crow," said Peijing, being practical.

"Yes, they built things much better in the old days," said Biju, as if she were much older than five. "The archer was just about to shoot the tenth and final sun out of the sky when his wife stopped him."

"Lucky thing. Otherwise we would have no suns left, and that would be a disaster," said Peijing.

"Women are smart," said Peijing, and they both nodded.

"I have made up a name for her," said Biju. "I'm going to call her the wise woman because it's a better name than just 'the archer's wife.' After all, she plays just as important a role in this story."

The sisters both nodded again.

CHAPTER SEVEN

Their new school was only a short walk across the park and then down the street, but Ba Ba drove them on the first day. Peijing sat in the back seat with Biju. She clutched her backpack tightly as the car pulled into the drop-off zone. She noticed a sign that said KISS AND GO, and she worried for a brief moment that something bad would happen if she didn't follow the exact instructions.

But she had never tried to kiss her parents before, and they had certainly never tried to kiss her. The Guo family were still very traditional and very Chinese and still held on to that concept of honor, even though they were in Australia now.

Some things were too old to let go of, and the new was still unfamiliar, so maybe all they could be right now was stuck in between. Like how Peijing felt, frozen because she couldn't bring herself to open the door, yet knew she couldn't stay in the car.

"Be good and listen to your teacher," said Ba Ba.

Peijing wanted to stay in the car a little longer. Maybe she would feel more ready if she had a bit more time. But Ba Ba was impatiently rolling and unrolling the big sheets of paper that contained all of his important plans. He had on his best suit and tie and kept checking his watch.

She stepped out of the car and tried to do it with conviction, to set a good example for Biju. Peijing watched as the car drove off, taking her sister with it. The kindergarten had a different entrance around the other side of the school. She wondered if the drop-off there had the same sign and whether Biju, even though she thankfully couldn't read yet, would figure out what the picture meant and try to kiss Ba Ba. Being small, Biju did not have a very good grasp of the concept of honor.

Peijing, on the other hand, understood that doing what the teacher asked of her and getting good grades would bring her honor.

Thinking about school brought her reality crashing back. The sight and sounds of all the other students flooding through the school entrance felt magnified and too close, too real. She hurried off to find her classroom on legs that felt like jelly, trying to count to five over and over in her head.

As Peijing had suspected, she could not help comparing everything to her previous school. This new school was in fact old, with discolored rusty patches on the weatherboard classrooms. Her old school had actually been new. She looked at the patchy grass and the giant trees with flesh-colored skin that peeled off in great sections. The weirdly confident birds that eyed her and gave low warning cries. She moved warily away from them.

It felt as though the inside of her head was spinning around like the colorful shapes inside one of those cardboard tubes you put your eye against. It had been mid-autumn when they had left Singapore, and here it was spring, heading into summer. But according to the books she had read, the leaves on the trees were supposed to be turning orange and falling off as it neared Christmas. None of these trees looked like their leaves were going to fall off regardless of the season.

Peijing located the classroom. Her new teacher, Miss Lena, introduced her to the students as Peijing stood there awkwardly hoping there was nothing out of place on her face or her hair or body. She kept worrying whether there was sleep between her eyes or a loose eyelash on her face or if her shirt was properly tucked in.

Once she was seated, Peijing started to feel more like part of the class, even though, instead of sitting in rows facing the front like at her old school, the desks were arranged to form a large rectangle and the class faced one another.

Nobody paid her much attention, but they seemed nice, and she was secretly relieved. Her greatest fear was that she would not fit in, that she would be picked on for looking different, because if she had a choice, she would love to look just like everyone else. She thought briefly about the lady at the school stationery store and scratched at an itchy spot on her knee.

It was also an odd feeling to be in a class with both girls and boys. Her old school had been only girls, all of them matching in their white blouses and pale blue pinafores. Peijing felt a slight embarrassment sitting there with a boy to her left, even though he ignored her just fine. On her other side was a thin girl with the wispiest, blondest hair she had ever seen.

Peijing drew both her hands into her lap and grasped them tightly. She tried not to look at the blond girl as it made her feel as if her thick black hair and tanned skin stuck out even more.

She felt shy, which got her thinking about how outgoing and popular she had been back at her school in Singapore, and how quickly this feeling changed. As if her whole personality had shifted for good and she could never get that better version of herself back again.

Miss Lena came over and asked if she was okay. Peijing nodded. Everything so far, if she had to sum it up, was a string of small, awkward experiences that she hoped would end soon.

It didn't make sense when Ba Ba had said this was the better education for both her and Biju. That he and Ma Ma thought it was a good idea that the whole family came with him when his company sent him to the new office in Australia. Maybe he should have just gone himself.

Peijing looked down at her black leather shoes, the ones all her old school friends wore, and then looked at the assortment of different-colored sneakers and shoelaces that bounced and kicked underneath the desks. Her mind whirled again with it all.

She almost didn't hear her teacher calling her name from the front of the class. She didn't even see Miss Lena until she was standing right in front of her. Peijing looked up, her eyes widened, and her mouth opened.

She braced herself for a stern talking-to. In her head the words *Sorry, Sister Lee!* and *I promise I'll pay more attention, Sister Lee!* swirled furiously. Her former teacher was very strict on manners and behavior. She even took out a ruler sometimes to measure how long your skirt was.

But that did not happen. Instead, Miss Lena spoke to her in a normal voice. In fact, the teacher looked concerned and worried for her.

"Peijing, do you mind stepping out of the class for a little while? Your sister, Biju, has requested you."

Oh! thought Peijing.

Peijing decided that although she always respected and obeyed the nuns at her old school, she really liked Miss Lena. She felt something in her heart that she had only ever felt for Ma Ma, Ba Ba, Ah Ma, and Biju. She felt like she wanted to be there at the new school because of Miss Lena.

Their teacher asked the tall girl who had come with the message to supervise the classroom while she was gone. Peijing followed Miss Lena out.

Down the slightly overgrown paths between the other classrooms and then across the teachers' carpark they went until they reached an even more outgrown area, where, nestled between the trees and painted blue, was a tiny wooden classroom on legs.

They both went inside, and Peijing took a good

look around. She didn't really know what to think. There was a lot to take in. There was a lot of stuff.

Not a single space on the walls wasn't covered in some sort of craft. Drying on a wire strung across the classroom were artworks made of sand and leaves and bark glued onto butcher's paper.

Ma Ma had always told her these things were "dirty" and that education was about letters and numbers on clean sheets of white paper. This classroom was foreign and unsettling and—Peijing wanted to think—wrong. But she couldn't bring herself to believe the last thought. Because as she touched the artworks and they wobbled on the wire, it made her feel joy.

Biju was sitting sadly in the corner with a red face and a downturned mouth. She looked up at Peijing, and her face became even sadder.

Miss Lena introduced Peijing to Mr. Brodie, the kindergarten teacher.

"She asked for you specifically," explained Mr. Brodie. "I thought if you talked to her, she might become more settled."

Peijing took a seat on the little plastic chair next to Biju and felt like a giant. If the teacher couldn't do anything about the situation, then what could she do? But that was something that Ma Ma would say. Peijing shook her mother out of her mind.

"What's wrong?" she whispered quietly to Biju. She looked around, feeling self-conscious she was speaking Chinese.

"I can't speak enough English," Biju replied. "I don't understand anyone; they don't understand me. I want to go home to Ah Ma."

Peijing was struck by a sense of responsibility that she wasn't prepared for.

"Everything's going to be okay," she said, even though her entire heart wasn't in it. "You will learn how to speak English. In fact, one day we will speak English all the time and the problem will be remembering how to speak Chinese!"

Biju shook her head and looked like she was going to cry.

"I promise everything's going to be okay," Peijing said again, hoping she didn't sound as empty as she felt. She changed the topic. "Hey, I like the craft hanging to dry on the wire. Did you do those this morning?"

Biju's frown turned into a smile then. "Yup! Can you imagine if we brought those bits of rubbish into our house? Ma Ma would have the biggest tantrum. Ha ha! I just want to see her face when the picture dries and I get to take it home."

"Then you have to stay until the end of class."

"I guess so," replied Biju, pursing her lips. "Only if you promise you'll watch Ma Ma's face when she comes to pick us up."

"I promise."

Biju looked a tiny bit happier.

"Everything's going to be okay," Peijing said again, desperate to make this clear to her little sister as she stood up to go. Somehow, she felt she was saying it more for herself.

"Thanks for having a word with her," said Mr. Brodie with a smile. Although Peijing did not smile back, she felt both happy and sad on the inside that everyone had been so kind to Biju.

Peijing watched as her sister crouched on the outer edge of the rug, where the other children sat waiting for a story. Biju watched them warily, like a five-hundred-year-old spirit from a folktale with the eyes of a five-year-old-child. Biju was tough and beyond her years, but she was also young, and her thoughts could be bent and shaped like lucky bamboo. She would survive. Thrive, even. Peijing wondered about herself.

"Are you okay?" Miss Lena asked again.

Peijing nodded.

Going back to class and leaving Biju was the hardest. Peijing stressed all the way back to the classroom and then stressed all through class. Those tummy feelings came back. She started resenting the fact that her sister had given her something extra to worry about. This new weight, added to her existing burden, was overwhelming.

Peijing looked out the window at the huge sky. So blue and yet so empty.

Miss Lena brought over a chair and sat across the desk from her. "How are you doing with the work?"

"It's okay," replied Peijing. The worksheet was easy enough; Peijing's class in Singapore had covered plate tectonics already. It was only hard because she couldn't really understand the English instructions very well and was sure she'd gotten most of it wrong. Her English was good, but as she had been learning how to read and write in Chinese at the same time, it wasn't as good as it should be.

"You can talk to me whenever you need to, okay?" said Miss Lena.

Peijing thought about how secretly scared she had been of Sister Lee. Not keeping up in class seemed like something to be ashamed of. She would never dare ask a question in front of the other students. But she felt that Miss Lena was being honest and wasn't trying to trick her to expose her weaknesses.

Miss Lena's curly hair was allowed to be wild and

free, even though a thought in Peijing's head—one that she didn't even know where it came from—told her Miss Lena should pull it back and have it in a neat bun. But her teacher's hair shone around her face, glorious like the sun.

Peijing also liked Miss Lena's soft blouse with the bow at the neck and the skirt that formed a fabric bubble around her knees, which seemed to reflect her personality.

"You can talk to me about the schoolwork," said Miss Lena. "And even about other things."

"Thank you," said Peijing. She was very appreciative that she could talk to Miss Lena if she ever needed to.

"Only one sun remained in the sky after the other nine were shot down and everyone celebrated," said Biju. "So, in his gratefulness, the king gifted an immortality pearl to the archer."

"Wait, the king has an immortality pearl just lying around?" asked Peijing.

"Well, this is the same kingdom afflicted by a dragon, a serpent, and an elephant-swallowing beast that all cried like babies, you know."

"I guess it's not out of the question, then," replied Peijing.

"But the celebrations were short-lived. The villagers were all fearful of an archer who was willing to shoot all the suns out of the sky."

CHAPTER EIGHT

Peijing did not want to sit by herself during lunch feeling the way she did. The kind voice of Miss Lena instructing the class through the learning activities had kept her soothed and distracted. Her worries about school had slowly faded. Being in the middle of it meant she was no longer scared of it, like being unafraid of the darkness of the playground at night when you are in the center holding on to a sparkler.

But, left alone, the thing that scared her most came flooding back.

Her thoughts.

To make things worse, she had checked her backpack, and there was no lunch there. Her familiar plastic lunch box with its little compartments inside was missing. Ma Ma must have forgotten.

Peijing's stomach rumbled in a sorry fashion, and

tears pricked her eyes. She had no choice but to sit in the lunch area with nothing to occupy her hands or her mind. She wasn't sure where to put her eyes.

Peijing tried to reassure herself that at least her mind had been diverted. She just wasn't sure having it diverted from one bad feeling to another was what she wanted.

She looked down at the concrete. It was miserable and gray. She stared at it long enough to be certain it was nothing more than miserable and gray and wasn't going to mercifully swallow her, and then she looked up.

At first, Peijing thought that the bright apparition in front of her was a celestial being, maybe the moon maiden herself. But then the figure moved to the side so that the sun was no longer behind their head. It was the girl with the wispy blond hair from class. When she smiled, a dimple appeared on her face. Only one dimple, even though she was smiling from cheek to cheek.

Peijing did not know why the girl was standing there. Maybe some of the other kids had put her up to this and it was a joke. Peijing's eyes darted suspiciously around the playground. She did not believe this lovely-looking girl truly and honestly wanted to be her friend. Maybe on the inside she didn't believe she deserved this girl to be her friend.

If I pretend she's not there or ignore her, maybe she'll go away, thought Peijing. There wasn't much to do without a lunch box, so Peijing ended up just weaving her fingers together and turning red. The girl stood there patiently and waited. She didn't go away.

"I like your unicorn clip," said Peijing after she couldn't stand it any longer. Ma Ma had drilled it into her to be polite all the time. Sometimes Peijing had hopeless daydreams of being wrongly arrested by the police one day, and all she would be able to say to them was "Thanks."

"You're nice," said the girl.

Peijing was caught off guard. For a moment, she believed the girl was talking about her personally, rather than just replying to a kind comment she had made just because she was obeying her mother.

"But it's not a unicorn," the girl went on. "It's a narwhal."

"What's a narwhal?"

"Unicorns aren't real, but narwhals are, and that's what makes them truly magical. They live in the Arctic waters, and one day I will be a narwhal scientist. My name is Joanna. Joanna Polonaise."

Peijing thought about the Little World. It did not have Arctic waters. Well, it was going to now, after she got home.

Joanna stuck one arm out and Peijing expected her to shake hands or give a high five because everyone liked shaking hands and high-fiving in Australia. Ba Ba said it was the local way. But the arm went across her body and she bowed deeply instead, a greeting that she seemed to have learned from somewhere not of this world or time.

Peijing gave a little nod in return.

"Where's your lunch?" Joanna asked, even though she didn't appear to have a lunch herself.

"My mother—" Peijing stopped abruptly. This was out of shock as behind Joanna, coming toward them, was Ma Ma herself. Carrying a three-layer tiffin lunch box.

Ma Ma approached and placed the tiffin on the ledge. Peijing hoped that Ma Ma would apologize for forgetting to pack lunch, and then just go. Instead, Ma Ma sat down next to the tiffin. She unlatched the handle and separated the three compartments. The contents let off a puff of steam and a pungent smell.

Ma Ma had not forgotten about lunch at all. She

was here to personally make sure it was delivered piping hot and that Peijing was going to eat the whole lot. Under her supervision.

"I can do this myself," Peijing said as Ma Ma prepared to push the piece of chicken between the chopsticks into her mouth.

"This will be quicker," replied Ma Ma.

"You didn't do this at my old school."

"I was confident about your old school. I'm not confident about this one."

Peijing turned her face away and squeezed her eyes shut.

She silently counted to five, her comforting lucky number.

When she opened her eyes, she was glad to see Ma Ma had rested the chopsticks back down. Peijing seized them and started shoveling the lunch into her mouth as quickly as she could.

She was aware that Joanna was still looking at her. She was aware that the other kids were looking at her as well. Nobody else had their mum personally turn up to feed them lunch.

Ma Ma, on the other hand, did not care about Joanna. And she certainly did not care about the other kids. Peijing wondered if she even cared much about herself these days as she was wearing an old shirt with a stain on the front.

Joanna just stood there, hovering like a pale, thin ghost.

Peijing was too afraid to be angry at Ma Ma, but she felt she had a right to be somewhat annoyed, and she was annoyed that Ma Ma was being really rude to Joanna by ignoring her. Whenever Peijing had faltered for just one moment in greeting one of Ma Ma's friends, Ma Ma would click her tongue and say, "Huh! Children these days have no manners!"

Well, if Peijing had no manners, she obviously got it from Ma Ma! She shoveled another ball of rice into her mouth.

She thought again how she was supposed to be a mirror of her mother and whether that meant she should start reflecting all the bad things about Ma Ma, not just the good things, and she felt a fire in her heart.

"You are going to affect your liver if you eat that fast," warned Ma Ma. "And I remind you not to run around afterward as it will give you appendicitis."

"Yes, I know," replied Peijing, even though she had learned during science class that running did not give anyone appendicitis.

Ma Ma was speaking in Chinese really loudly.

Peijing was being as polite as she could, replying back in Chinese when all she wanted to do was blend in and speak English. And not have Ma Ma there.

"Hurry up and finish eating so that I can go feed Biju," said Ma Ma.

But you just told me to not eat too fast, Peijing wanted to scream in frustration. But she did not say anything. She just put her chopsticks down and said that she was full.

"No. You have to eat everything," said Ma Ma.

Peijing picked up her chopsticks and quickly (but not too quickly) ate everything. The chicken, the vegetables, the steamed white rice. She felt sick. The food sat uncomfortably on top of her anxiety and pressed down on her gut.

"Good," said Ma Ma, and she stacked the empty compartments back together, secured the tiffin, and left.

All the kids were staring now. Some were elbowing each other in the ribs and snickering and pointing and others pretended not to hear. But no one told anyone else to stop making fun of her.

"Sorry," mumbled Peijing to Joanna. Once again, she imagined the scenario of police arresting her for something she did not do and this time her only word being *Sorry*.

"Isn't that lovely of your mum?" exclaimed Joanna, bursting with enthusiasm. "My mother would never care enough to do anything like that! If she did, well, she wouldn't have gone away and left me with Dad."

Peijing wanted to open her mouth and say something nice, but she looked at the suddenly down-turned expression on Joanna's face. She closed her mouth. It wouldn't work to talk in two different languages of sadness.

She knew the girl could never understand her, just like she couldn't understand the life of this girl. But she was glad she was still standing there. She couldn't explain it, but she felt a kinship with Joanna. Like they had something in common even though they were obviously two completely different people.

"What is your star sign?" asked Joanna.

"I'm a rabbit," replied Peijing.

Joanna frowned. "I don't think that is a star sign. I'm a Pisces. Two fish swimming in the opposite direction."

Peijing shook her head. She was sure there were no fish in the Chinese zodiac. There was a dragon, which sometimes swam underwater, but it was not a fish. Again, it felt as though they were talking about the same thing, but that their versions of the same thing were different.

"Can I show you something?" asked Joanna.

Peijing nodded.

"Then come with me." Joanna held out her hand.

Peijing put her hand into the girl's, the one she had nothing in common with, and away they went.

"The villagers were in a real panic because nobody wanted an archer with an immortality pearl that went around shooting suns down, not when there was only one left," said Biju.

"I would worry too," said Peijing.

"I know, right?" Biju's voice was excitable. "Imagine if you were scared of the dark!"

"So, the wise woman decided to steal the immortality pearl. The Archer found out and started chasing her. He was gaining ground. She did the only thing she could to stop him getting it back."

"What did she do?" asked Peijing.

"She swallowed the pearl."

CHAPTER NINE

Peijing followed Joanna, who took her away from the school and across the oval where the big kids were trying to play football and cricket at the same time.

"Look at this," said Joanna.

Peijing was too nervous to look. They had stopped now. But they had also passed the school border by the length of both of their arms held out, fingertip to fingertip. She would feel much better if they were back on the safe side.

"I think it must be a magical door—what do you think?" asked Joanna. She didn't seem fussed, as though she did this thing all the time. Peijing was starting to suspect she did. Joanna didn't seem to have any friends, so maybe this is where she came to sit every lunch break.

"Maybe it leads to a different dimension," Joanna continued.

"What is a dimension?" asked Peijing. "My English is not very good," she added hastily. Her cheeks reddened.

"Oh, it's the same as a different world, really," said Joanna.

"Why don't you just say 'different world,' then?"

"I don't know," said Joanna. "The English language is weird."

Peijing could understand. She thought about her friend Yifen, whose last name, Jiang, was a very noble one that meant "river." Unfortunately, it also sounded like another Jiang that meant "hopping chi-sucking vampire," so sometimes she got teased. Chinese was a weird language too.

But Peijing did not want to think about Yifen. She could not be where Yifen was right now; she couldn't help her if anyone was making fun of her.

Peijing sighed and finally looked up at the giant old tree. It was a sorry thing. Peijing couldn't tell if it was dead or still clinging on. It had only one green leaf left. Mostly it was just a giant trunk with a huge, gaping black hole that made a doorway.

The doorway was exactly Peijing and Joanna's height.

"Have you not been inside it before?" Peijing asked.

"No," said Joanna.

"Let's go inside."

"I don't want to spoil the magic if it turns out to be just a tree!"

Peijing ignored her and stepped through the hole. It was dark, and she spread her arms out. She touched the inside of the tree. It was surprisingly sharp, and she pulled away with a drawn breath. She put her hands out again and felt the entire way around. It did not lead to further magical lands or dimensions. It was just a tree that managed to keep standing despite being completely hollow.

"Are you still there?" Joanna called from outside.

Peijing put an arm out. She felt Joanna take her hand, and she pulled the girl in.

"Oh," said Joanna. "It's just a tree."

Peijing crossed her legs and sat down on the soft bed of leaves. Joanna did too.

"I haven't heard from my mum since she went away when I was little," Joanna started saying in the darkness. "Her last words were, 'I'm just going to the shops—do you want sliced chicken or ham for your school sandwiches?' Now I live with just my dad. I don't have any siblings. I'm really lonely."

"We moved here because of my dad's job," said Peijing. "I have a little sister, but she's really annoying. Although I have the both of them and my mother and grandmother as well, I feel lonely too."

It was then that Peijing realized that just because the tree did not lead to a different land (or dimension), it didn't mean it wasn't magic. Sitting with Joanna in the small dark place, their knees touching, she felt a deep and special connection with her. The motes of dust floating through the air seemed like particles of gold as they passed through the light of the entryway.

"My favorite dinner is apricot chicken. What about yours?" Joanna asked.

"Black bean chicken."

They looked at each other, doubting if the other's choice sounded appetizing.

"What's your favorite color? Mine is blue," Joanna said.

"I like pink," said Peijing.

They were just so different.

"Are we friends?" asked Joanna.

"We are friends," said Peijing.

But they felt right together.

And maybe that was the most special magic of them all.

Peijing and Joanna smiled at each other. Their smiles were the same.

Ma Ma picked up Biju and Peijing after shool. As Ma Ma didn't know how to drive, they walked home. Biju delighted in showing Ma Ma the artwork she had made with the bark, leaves, and sand stuck to it. Just as predicted, Ma Ma took one look, said that it was "dirty," and deposited it straight into a trash bin on the sidewalk.

Peijing could see another child showing her mother the same artwork. "That's lovely," said the mother. Peijing could tell by the mother's face she did not really mean it. But she still pretended and put on a show. Peijing immediately wanted to get angry at this parent because the parent was lying, and lying did not teach you to do better work or get better grades. She wanted to . . . but she just couldn't.

Biju grinned and gave a big "Huh!" of a laugh, but Peijing caught her sneaking a look back at the trash bin with a mournful expression on her face, before she went back to the act of making believe that she didn't care.

Peijing watched her sister carefully as they crossed the park, but Biju seemed to have become distracted by the sky, the grass, the dogs on their walks. She would run off into the distance and run back for no reason other than that she was chasing life.

"I'm going to be a movie star!" declared Biju loudly after a while. "I've decided that when I grow up, I'm going to be famous. I'm going to live in a great big mansion and have a great big car and everyone is going to love me. If you want to love me too, then you'd just have to line up."

"I don't think Ma Ma would want you to be a movie star," replied Peijing. She said it quietly, watching the back of Ma Ma's head in front of them. When did Ma Ma have so many gray hairs?

"She will change her mind when she sees me acting. Our class is going to be doing a play. I am going to audition for the princess. I get kidnapped by a dragon and saved by a knight. It is the most important role in the whole play."

"That's good," said Peijing absentmindedly.

"You will come and see me as the princess in the play, won't you?" said Biju, stopping and clinging onto her sister's arm.

"Of course," Peijing replied, suddenly worried by the fact Biju had stopped moving. "If I get invited."

Biju started running ahead again, and Peijing felt relieved.

Then she came back.

"Ma Ma and Ba Ba will come watch too, won't they?" The words came out so quietly that it was hardly a whisper. Once again, she stopped, her hands heavy on Peijing's arm.

Peijing did not want to lie to Biju.

But she didn't want to tell her the painful truth: that her parents wouldn't come and watch the play. That they just wanted their daughters to study and get A grades, and everything else was considered a waste of time.

Pejing remembered when she was around Biju's age, when she got the role of Mother Bear in *Goldilocks and the Three Bears* and neither Ma Ma nor Ba Ba showed up. Luckily, she was wearing a paper plate mask that hid the tears streaming down her face.

"Ba Ba will be at work, and Ma Ma has a lot to do around the house," Peijing said, choosing her words carefully.

"What could be more important than me?" Biju replied really loudly and ran off. She didn't come back to Peijing this time; she ran straight ahead until they reached home.

"Nothing," Peijing should have replied, but she thought it too late. The moment had passed.

FULL MOON

"As soon as she swallowed the pearl, the wise woman became so light she started to float toward the moon."

"Oh!" said Peijing.

"But the archer tried to shoot her down," said Biju.

"He did not!" Peijing spoke loudly in indignation, even though she was not usually one for passionate displays. She didn't want Ma Ma to think she was having a bout of "heatiness" and then boil her a horrible medicinal soup made out of monk fruit and white fungus to cool her yin energy down.

"But every one of his arrows missed."

"Well, thank goodness for that. Men!" shouted Peijing. It took something important to make Peijing shout.

The two sisters stared and nodded at each other as though they were old enough to know all about boys.

CHAPTER TEN

There was a special test today at school. Miss Lena had a boom box set up on her desk and she was dancing with excitement. She explained that anyone who passed would be invited to join a special after-school music program. They would hear a series of musical bursts and had to choose from a multiple-choice selection.

"I will do terribly," said Joanna. "My dad always tells me I'm deaf."

Peijing concentrated on her questions.

How many different instruments can you hear at the same time?

The music clip played.

Peijing could hear five different instruments.

She went to mark the answer down, and then she broke out in a sweat. Who was going to take her to after-school music class? Ba Ba? No. Ma Ma? No.

Did her parents even approve of after-school music class? She knew they only approved of school.

She looked down at the question again, and, with a shaking hand, she marked down four.

Peijing continued with the entire test and made sure that her answers were all wrong, until she thought the person marking it might get suspicious, so she made sure she got a few she thought were right. When it was over, she flipped her paper upside down and pushed it away from her, all the way to the corner of her desk.

"My dad is wrong," said Joanna. "I'm not deaf at all."

Miss Lena was inspired by the test to talk about musical instruments, *Peter and the Wolf*, and how she used to date someone in a famous rock band when she was twenty-one. The rest of the class was enraptured, but Peijing didn't have the stomach to listen to her stories. Today was not the first scene in a movie where she discovered that she had a hidden musical talent and played the cello for a world-class orchestra.

"Are you okay, Peijing?" asked Miss Lena as she came around handing out slips to the students.

Peijing nodded and smiled up at her teacher. It was a genuine smile intended for Miss Lena.

"This will cheer you up," said Miss Lena and gave her a pink slip of paper.

Peijing looked at it. It said:

> *Join us for a wonderful week of fun filled days and magical nights under the stars in the Western Australian Wildflower Country.*

"Oh, gosh, I hope I can go!" exclaimed Joanna.

"Me too," said Peijing, glad to agree with her friend.

But on the inside, she braced herself and practiced saying it wasn't a big deal if she wasn't allowed to go.

"What is this?" asked Ma Ma, frowning at the slip of paper in her hands.

"Camping," said Peijing breathlessly. "Our whole year is going. Can I please go? You just need to sign the slip. And give Miss Lena the money."

"No," said Ma Ma.

"Why?" said Peijing. "Everyone is going."

"You have a perfectly good home and bed. Why do you want to sleep in a tent?" said Ma Ma. It wasn't really an explanation.

But Ma Ma's word was final, and there were to be no more questions, protesting, or tears. Ma Ma dropped the slip in the trash bin, and Peijing couldn't help but look at it, sitting faceup. She watched as cooking scraps and rubbish were placed on top of it, smudging the ink and ruining the slip until it eventually became buried.

Ba Ba liked to eat his dinner piping hot. It had to be fresh, never reheated. And if it wasn't on the table when he came home starving after a long day at work, he got grumpy. So the act of Ba Ba stepping through the front door was a countdown fraught with excitement and mild pandemonium.

Ma Ma would fuss around the kitchen, setting into motion the final cooking stages—tossing vegetables into the wok, clicking the rice cooker back on to warm. Peijing asked once if she could help, but Ma Ma just clicked her tongue and told her to stop getting in the way.

When dinner was finally assembled, Ba Ba was home, and everyone sat down, Peijing would breathe out a sigh of relief and secretly thank all the gods responsible, amazed that something that felt so precarious could be pulled together in the end.

It was her favorite time of the day. She would

study Ba Ba, Ma Ma, Ah Ma, and Biju in turn and feel lucky that she had a family. Today she thought about Joanna and her mother, who went to the shops to buy slices of chicken and never came back.

"I would like to come along for the walk to the girls' school tomorrow," said Ah Ma.

"We already talked about this," replied Ma Ma. "The doctor back in Singapore said you were only to do tai chi for exercise and not put unnecessary pressure on your knees."

Peijing did not like how Ah Ma only replied with a sad face.

"Please use your chopsticks properly," Ma Ma said to Biju.

Biju stopped mucking around with them and instead stabbed them upright into her bowl of rice, so they stood like two joss sticks intended for the dead. Ba Ba cleared his throat. Biju looked up.

Then she silently left her seat and padded toward the kitchen. Everyone sat at the table without saying anything until Biju returned.

With a fork and a spoon.

Biju started eating her rice with a spoon.

"What are you doing?" said Ma Ma.

"I am eating my rice with a spoon," replied Biju simply.

Oh, no, thought Peijing. Biju was practically asking for discipline with the chicken feather duster.

"I have always wondered myself why anyone would choose to eat hundreds of tiny rice grains with two sticks," said Ah Ma. "But as the proverb goes, He who wishes to move a mountain starts by shifting small stones."

Peijing exchanged a look with Ah Ma. She couldn't help but smile.

Ma Ma, though, did not smile.

"Please explain why you are eating with a spoon."

Biju leaned over the table and stabbed a piece of broccoli with her fork.

"And a fork," added Ma Ma.

"I'm not going to use chopsticks anymore," declared Biju. "I am going to use a spoon and a fork like everyone else at school."

"That's not how things are in this family. Please put your fork down and use your chopsticks," Ma Ma said.

"No," said Biju.

"Biju! You are to leave this table until you learn some manners!" shouted Ma Ma and stood up.

Biju got out of her seat, burst into tears, and ran off in the direction of their bedroom.

Ma Ma sat down again and was irritated for the

rest of dinner. Ba Ba did not say a single word. Peijing wanted to go after Biju, but she knew better than to try to do anything that would annoy Ma Ma further.

So she sat there and obediently ate her dinner. Something inside of her wanted to behave even more honorably for Ma Ma, almost as if she was making up for Biju. She asked Ma Ma if she wanted help with washing the dishes, but Ma Ma told her again that she would only get in the way.

Suddenly, Peijing thought of a different Biju. The one looking small and withdrawn in the corner of her classroom on the first day of school, who had asked to see her big sister. A strong sense of protectiveness surged through her. Biju was only a child. Peijing thought about Ma Ma yelling at Biju and Ba Ba saying nothing, and felt a strange feeling she couldn't quite put into words.

It wasn't until she was sitting with Biju in their bedroom, trying to get her sister to stop facing the wall and talk to her, that she realized what it was. She was mad at her parents. Peijing pushed the thought aside immediately. She didn't dare entertain such an idea in her head, even to herself; her hands crept up to her face and gently slapped at her closed mouth.

It was an instantaneous habit born from old, superstitious beliefs. Something she had grown up doing and that all her cousins and friends also did, after uttering or thinking something unlucky or evil or bad. Peijing told herself on the spot that now that they were in Australia she wasn't going to do it anymore.

"So, the wise woman floated all the way to the moon, where she became a goddess, with no one for company except the jade rabbit, who makes the elixir of life to keep her young."

"What?" interrupted Peijing. "The immortality pearl didn't keep her immortal forever?"

"I didn't invent this folktale; it's thousands of years old," said Biju, cranky that her sister chose to focus on the unimportant bits of the story. "Anyway, the moral of the story is that the wise woman did an honorable deed to protect the people from the potentially dangerous archer and was rewarded."

Peijing wondered why every single Chinese myth was about honor and why honor was so important anyway.

CHAPTER ELEVEN

It was no good; Biju refused to talk to her. So, annoyed at her own helplessness, Peijing sighed loudly, got up, and left the room.

"She is too rebellious!" Peijing heard Ma Ma complaining to Ba Ba in the kitchen.

Peijing pressed herself against the wall and willed herself to be unseen as she passed down the hallway. She made it to the living room and squeezed herself onto the couch next to Ah Ma. Ah Ma was watching the Hong Kong weather channel on the satellite TV. Peijing felt embarrassed at the sight of Ah Ma staring mindlessly at the dancing pictures of suns and rain clouds and turned it to the news channel instead.

"Why can't Biju use a spoon or a fork if she wants to?" burst forth the question from Peijing's lips.

Ah Ma turned her kind eyes toward Peijing and

gave her a wise smile. "What is your name again, young child?"

"It's me, Peijing," she replied, feeling confused. Could Ah Ma not see her properly in the half dark?

"Oh, yes, so it is, my *sunnu*. What is your question for Ah Ma?"

"I just want to know why Biju is not allowed to use a spoon or a fork if she wants to. Is it such a big deal?"

Ah Ma seemed to focus on the television screen, and Peijing thought she might have lost her again, but then her grandmother turned back.

"A spoon or a fork is very easy to use. Chopsticks, on the other hand, are very hard. If you stop using them while you are still young, one day when you are old you might realize you have forgotten how."

Peijing thought about her grandmother's words carefully.

"As the old proverb goes, 'One step in the wrong direction will cause you a thousand years of regret,'" said Ah Ma. She beamed at Peijing.

Peijing put her hand on top of Ah Ma's.

Ah Ma put her other hand on top of Peijing's, and they held each other.

"You are very wise."

"Oh, I'm just old." Ah Ma chuckled. "You pick up a few things here and there when you live this long."

It was true: Ah Ma was really old. She had stopped having birthdays a long time ago. It was bad luck to flaunt her old age, just in case the heavens noticed and decided it was time to take her back.

Peijing tiptoed back into the kitchen, glad to see Ba Ba and Ma Ma had gone. Standing at the sink, she picked up a pair of bamboo chopsticks drying in the dish drainer. She placed them between her fingers and, with a newfound appreciation, she levered them up and down, admiring the swift motions. From the countertop she snagged a dried red bean that had escaped being cooked and was hiding along the edge of the window. She brought it up to her eye and stared at it, and for a moment the world felt right.

Back in their bedroom, Peijing found Ba Ba sitting on the bed, while Biju, cross-legged and with arms folded, was still facing the wall.

"You just need to be a good girl and listen to Ma Ma!"

Ba Ba looked up at Peijing as she came into the room, but he did not smile. In fact, Peijing could not quite place the last time she saw Ba Ba smile.

He never smiled at the dinner table. He didn't smile when Peijing got a good report card that was mostly As. He didn't smile when Peijing hand-sewed him a necktie at school for Father's Day. She had never seen him wear the necktie, suspected he had thrown it away a long time ago.

Peijing was surprised to see him trying to talk to Biju, something he hadn't done since the morning when Biju's ear was cut. Ba Ba's job had always been working at the office, not helping to raise the kids at home. He never got up in the middle of the night when they were babies, and he certainly never changed a diaper, as Ma Ma liked to remind them all.

"Do you understand, Biju?" asked Ba Ba, even though it sounded more like an order than a question. Then he got up and left, without giving either of them another glance.

Peijing could tell by the way Biju was holding herself that, even though her sister said nothing, she actually had a lot to say. It was just all bottled up inside of her, the lid screwed on tightly by her pride.

So Peijing dragged out the cardboard box from underneath her bed. The world was bountiful, and new species were emerging almost daily. She thought about Joanne and the Arctic sea and narwhals. Peijing angled herself so her back was to Biju and made a lot of interesting rustling noises. It wasn't long before she felt a warm breath upon her neck.

"It is so unfair! What makes Ma Ma thinks she can set the rules? Why is she always right? If she is so right, how come not a single person in my class eats with chopsticks?" Biju was a small typhoon. "And you know what? I am sick of Ma Ma's cooking! Do you know what I want to eat? What everyone said they were having for dinner when we went around the circle today. Fish and chips! Chicken nuggets!"

Peijing let Biju's feelings all come out, until Biju was lost for words and became quiet again.

"Ma Ma doesn't want you to forget how to use chopsticks, that's all. I think that's reasonable enough," said Peijing. She knew they had only been in Australia for two weeks, but life's lessons seemed like they faded so easily. She was sure she had forgotten already what the symbol on the top of Ah Ma's mooncake looked like.

"Who cares? I don't care if I never use them again! I'd rather use my fingers first! And eat a double cheeseburger."

Biju flopped down on the bed and stared at the ceiling.

"Maybe one day," said Peijing with a sense of wistfulness, thinking of what Ah Ma would say, "you will look back and wish for something that you used to have. But it will be too late then."

Biju kept staring at the ceiling. "I wish we were back home," she said.

Peijing did not have a counterargument for that because she missed home too.

"Let's get into our pajamas and have a teeth-brushing contest! Whoever can hold the foam in their mouth longest wins," she said, changing the topic.

Biju concentrated all her energy into the contest as she was very competitive. She certainly got that from Ma Ma. Or from what Ma Ma used to be, anyway. Peijing tried to put the same effort into it, but her heart just wasn't there. She was glad she had distracted Biju. But come tomorrow her sister would forget all about what utensil she was supposed to use for dinner. She'd use her chopsticks again and be looking for her next challenge, the next fight to pick.

Peijing, on the other hand, knew that she would carry this memory inside of her for a long time. She thought about the last time when things felt right, back on the night of the Mid-Autumn Festival. It felt so long ago.

"The archer still missed the goddess down on earth, so when the moon was round, he left her gifts of cakes and sweets outside, so she could see them," said Biju. "One of her favorites was an egg yolk wrapped in pastry. So that is why we make mooncakes during Mid-Autumn Festival. Ah Ma told me."

"I would never forgive him for trying to shoot me down with arrows," said Peijing, full of honor even though she claimed she wasn't.

"Adults are funny things," said Biju. "I said the same thing to Ah Ma, and she just told me it was a matter of the heart. Whatever that means."

"Ah Ma told me that the Mid-Autumn Festival is also when all daughters who live away return to their parents," said Peijing.

"Except for the goddess. She can never return," said Biju sadly.

CHAPTER TWELVE

Last year, a school fundraiser that sold an awful lot of car washes and cakes had helped the aging school buy a brand-new art wing. Through the windows on the ceiling that could be wound up to let fresh air in, Peijing could see blue skies in safe, contained squares.

She thought about the art portfolio she had left behind at school in Singapore. She thought about how she had gotten perfect marks and yet Ma Ma had never been interested in seeing a single project from it. She thought about her art teacher asking if she wanted to take it home on her last day and how she shook her head. She never found out what they did with her art portfolio.

In her backpack, Peijing still had the leaflet she had taken from the school supplies store next door, the one about the Look Before You Dive poster competition.

Peijing had been convincing herself that maybe, just maybe, if she won the poster competition, Ma Ma would be wrong in saying that drawing wasn't worthwhile. And maybe, just maybe, she might look at her own work and not be so critical of herself.

Before she lost the courage, she flattened the scrunched-up leaflet and showed it to Miss Elizabeth, the art teacher. Miss Elizabeth studied it carefully with her large tortoiseshell glasses and then smiled at Peijing and said that it sounded like an ideal activity for the class to do. Peijing walked back to her desk smiling, but also shaking.

Miss Elizabeth handed out a large A3 sheet of paper to each of the students and passed around the competition leaflet, telling them how important it was to prevent spinal injury because it was usually irreversible, and you'd never be the same again. That if they won a certificate, it would make the school proud. Peijing quivered at the challenge of fulfilling another honor, but her heart told her she wanted to win.

The class didn't have any questions about spinal injury or the importance of making the school proud, they just wanted to know what the mystery prizes to be won were. Miss Elizabeth told them that mysteries were supposed to be mysterious.

Peijing picked up a lead pencil and then hesitated. She realized she hadn't drawn people for a long time. Only moons, the natural world, and every animal that ever existed. There wasn't a single person in the Little World.

Once, her friend Yifen's mother, who was a respected artist in the traditional Chinese form, had tried to give Peijing pointers. It was disastrous. All Peijing could remember was Mrs. Jiang telling her about hands. It was all in the hands. You could truly tell if a drawing was good or not by the way the way the artist drew the hands. Mrs. Jiang's voice had been as sharp as the ruler she brandished.

Peijing felt her own hand clench the pencil so tight that she couldn't release it even if she wanted to.

"Just do your best, love," said Miss Elizabeth as she paused by Peijing's desk. "It's not a contest. No, actually, it is. But you know what I mean!"

Peijing had never been called "love" before. She stared at her art teacher as Miss Elizabeth made her way between the desks, chatting to the students. Feeling heartened, she touched her pencil against the blank paper and slowly formed a face.

She drew a beach scene and so many people. She drew people doing the right thing, people enjoying themselves, people involved in smaller stories inside the bigger story—where a group of children were getting ready to dive off a pier with hidden rocks below. Peijing drew a thick red circle around them with a big red cross.

Her shoulders started to loosen. She was actually enjoying this, even though some of her people had hands that looked a lot like cauliflower. Her fingers relaxed.

There was a heavy feeling on her arm.

Peijing put her pencil down and glanced over. Joanna had fallen asleep pressed against her.

"Wake up! Are you okay?"

Joanna stirred. Her stomach replied for her by giving an awfully loud growl. It was so loud some of the other students turned around and laughed. Joanna sighed and picked up her pencil. Materializing in front of her was a sad person with a downturned mouth in a hospital bed, wrapped tightly from head to toe in bandages. IF YOU WANT TO STAY ALIVE, LOOK BEFORE YOU DIVE! shouted the big red bubble letters.

"I'm fine," said Joanna.

Peijing knew Joanna was thin, but up close the girl's hand, resting on the desk next to hers, was no more than a pale piece of skin stretched over bone. Peijing's eyes followed the hand up to the equally bony arm, and she stared at Joanna's jutting collarbone. She guessed she had been too wrapped up in her own world to notice before.

Joanna did up the top button on her school top. Peijing turned back to her own work, embarrassed at herself.

Joanna didn't speak after that. She just worked determinedly on her poster, carefully cleaning up the edges with an eraser. Peijing admired the hands of Joanna's hospital patient, the only things exposed under the bandages. The fingers were neat and realistic; they did not look unintentionally like string beans.

Peijing didn't think her own work was any good, after all. Maybe that's why Ma Ma kept throwing away everything she made for the Little World; Ma Ma thought her drawings were awful.

The silence between her and Joanna had only lasted a quarter of an hour, but to Peijing it felt as though multiple suns and moons had passed overhead.

"Are we still going to the tree at lunchtime?" she burst out saying.

"We can," replied Joanna.

"That would make me really happy. I hope you're still my friend."

Joanna yawned and, from behind them, Peijing

could hear Joanna's name being whispered and then more laughter. Joanna, though, didn't seem to be able to concentrate on herself, let alone be aware of what other people thought of her.

Peijing did not understand why the other students were making fun of Joanna; she'd thought that, with her long blond hair and blue eyes, Joanna was one of them. She felt a wave of protectiveness wash over her, similar to how she felt whenever she thought about Biju. It was different sort of attachment, and hard to explain. Not a matter of the mind, but a matter of the heart. The feeling echoed like a story she might have heard once.

Miss Elizabeth collected all their posters at the end of class. She said that Peijing did a great job, and Peijing felt better about herself. She had honestly tried the best she could. She asked herself if she would have still drawn the same picture even if she knew she wouldn't win, and the answer was yes. She felt so whole whenever she drew.

Walking back to Miss Lena's class from Miss Elizabeth's art classroom, untethered for a brief moment to no teacher, the kids started becoming chatty and rowdy. Peijing found Joanna bumping into her suddenly, almost knocking her off her feet.

Peijing was okay, but her feelings were hurt. Until she realized that someone had pushed Joanna—on purpose—and her friend had wheeled around in fright. Peijing caught her. Joanna's fingers curled around hers, and she let Peijing hold her hand the rest of the way back.

Miss Lena handed their worksheets on plate tectonics back, and Peijing was not surprised that she hadn't done very well, but it took her a while to figure out as she was looking for the big red crosses that weren't there. Miss Lena had used a purple pen to mark instead, and she had made the ticks large, but the crosses really small.

Peijing was happy to pass. Even though she should have gotten one hundred percent as she had already covered the topic in Singapore, she had guessed rightly that it was the English that had tripped her up. Peijing thought about Ma Ma and how Ma Ma wouldn't understand; she would just be angry and think Peijing was making up excuses.

"Would you like to go through the answers later? We can even do it during lunch. I just want to understand how much you know," said Miss Lena. "Same with you, Joanna."

Peijing was confused about what Miss Lena was talking about. Until she looked over at Joanna's worksheet and realized Joanna had done even worse than she had.

"How did you get a lower score than me?" Peijing hissed to Joanna after Miss Lena was gone. "Aren't you supposed to be able to understand English?"

"I don't know," said Joanna.

Peijing didn't want to accept that as an answer, so she kept staring.

"Maybe I'm just dumb," Joanna snapped. "Are you happy?"

Peijing could feel Joanna withdraw from her, and she was sorry.

"I didn't mean to get mad," Joanna said in a gentler voice. "Sometimes I just find it hard to concentrate at school when I'm hungry." Joanna was sorry too.

Each part of the puzzle that was supposed to be an answer for Peijing was turning out to be another question. She didn't know quite what to say. She hoped that by just being the person sitting next to her, a friend, somehow Joanna would feel some comfort.

"I have another story. Ma Ma told me this one," said Biju. "Even though Ma Ma's stories can be a bit—"

"Shhh," said Peijing. "Let me hear it."

"Once upon a time, there lived a boy who had a kind heart but who had no parents and no home. He met an old beggar woman one day and, because he was lonely, asked her if she would be his grandmother."

"That is sad," said Peijing, who had a soft heart even though she didn't want to admit it. "Did she say yes?"

"She did," said Biju. "And she gave him a tiny wooden boat and said that a great flood would be coming soon. 'Keep the boat safe and make one promise to me. You will only rescue animals. Never a human.'"

"Why's that?" asked Peijing.

"The lesson will come later," said Biju firmly. "The sun shone for one hundred days straight. But then it started to rain. And rain and rain."

CHAPTER THIRTEEN

It was lunchtime, and Ma Ma was back, gripping the tiffin with the determined expression of someone with the single goal of getting her daughter fed. Once again Joanna stood there like a pale ghost at a respectful distance, but close enough for Peijing to notice, for the first time, how battered the girl's leather shoes were. The sole on the bottom of one of them hung open like a sad mouth. This led her to notice that one of Joanna's socks was longer than the other and that, upon inspection, they were in fact completely different socks. Peijing was too polite to say anything.

Ma Ma unstacked all the tiffin compartments, and Peijing started eating. Like the day before, she got the same glances from the other kids, the same snickers. Peijing couldn't help feeling deeply embarrassed, even as she chomped away at the food and enjoyed it. She didn't know where to look, and her eyes, darting around, locked onto Joanna's. Joanna gave her a nod, as if she understood.

It made Peijing think about Ah Ma's words from last night, how Ah Ma had spoken about regret and realizing things too late. Suddenly, Peijing understood clearly.

She told herself that Ma Ma cared about her enough to cook her a hot lunch and walk all the way from home and back again. The tragedy was that if she didn't learn to appreciate it now, one day she would look back and want to thank Ma Ma, only to find Ma Ma was not there to bring her lunch anymore.

Miss Lena, doing the lunchtime patrol, walked past and smiled at them.

Joanna shifted on one foot and then the other. It was then that it occurred to Peijing to ask, "Where is your lunch?"

Come to think of it, she hadn't seemed to have a lunch yesterday, either.

Joanna picked at an imaginary piece of lint on her shirt.

"Sometimes my dad forgets. He has a bad memory, that's all."

Peijing patted the space on the ledge next to her,

and Joanna edged closer like a wary stray cat. Then she sat down.

Peijing was worried that Joanna would say her food smelled disgusting. Or, when she was handed some, that she wouldn't want it after all because it looked funny. But Joanna just stared curiously at the chopsticks Peijing passed to her, and she used one of them to stab a fried square of tofu. The girl ate everything in her tiffin, even all the vegetables.

"That is the nicest meal I've ever had," Joanna declared afterward and for a moment Peijing thought she was going to lick the container. Then she burped loudly and wiped her face with the back of her hand.

Peijing looked at Ma Ma. Ma Ma looked back at Peijing, then she looked at Joanna. More accurately, she looked at Joanna's left shoe. From her handbag, which seemed to hold all matter of bits and pieces and random things that might come in handy—like little packets of chili sauce and napkins stolen from *kopi tiams*—Ma Ma took out a green rubber band, the ones that held together bunches of bok choy from the markets back in Singapore.

She wrapped it around Joanna's shoe to hold the sole back against the bottom of the shoe.

"That's much better," said Joanna.

Ma Ma just nodded. She still looked at the girl with a level of suspicion.

"Okay, you can go now," said Peijing, quickly stacking up the empty containers and securing the tiffin together. As much as she respected her mother, she also respected the fact there was a magic tree that needed to be visited before the bell rang.

Ma Ma was up on her feet and walking across the undercover lunch area when the teacher on lunch duty, one that Peijing had never seen before, started approaching from the other end. Sensing trouble, Peijing rushed over. Joanna followed.

"Excuse me, but you are not allowed on the school premises without permission," the teacher said to Ma Ma.

"What is this woman saying?" Ma Ma asked Peijing in Chinese.

"She says you are not allowed to be here," said Peijing to Ma Ma back in Chinese.

"Excuse me, we only speak English at this school," said the teacher.

"But I have to speak to my mother in Chinese," Peijing explained. "She doesn't understand English."

"I don't think she's speaking to her mum in Chinese to keep a secret from you," said Joanna chiming in, hoping to help. It made the teacher look even madder.

"I can tell when I'm unwanted," Ma Ma said coldly, and she marched away.

"Can we go now, Miss Sara?" Joanna asked the teacher.

"I will remind you we only speak English at this school," Miss Sara repeated, looking directly at Peijing. Peijing felt her face burning with shame.

"I don't know how to speak Chinese, so I promise I won't do it!" Joanna replied. Then she wrapped her hand around Peijing's and they were off. Away from the classrooms and across the oval and past the school border by the length of two arms, touching fingertip to fingertip. They did not stop until they ducked inside the tree, the dust motes making them sneeze, but looking like magic.

"Miss Sara is just a bully sometimes!" said Joanna inside the safety of the tree.

"What did you say to Miss Sara?" asked Peijing. She thought she had heard right, but she was stunned all the same.

"I told her I promised not to speak Chinese!"

"But you talked back . . . to a . . . teacher." Peijing couldn't help but whisper the last word.

"Grown-ups can sometimes be wrong," replied Joanna. "Sometimes you got to fight for your rights!" Then she grinned. Joanna was standing up with her hands on her hips, and the light coming in on her yellow hair made it look like gold. Peijing was suddenly inspired to put her hands on her hips, and stand like a superhero too.

Joanna started laughing. Peijing started laughing too.

"Tell me about those cubes your mother cooked—what is that?"

"Tofu," said Peijing.

"Ha, tofu," repeated Joanna with a thoughtful expression on her face. "I don't know how to spell it, but I like the taste of it."

Toward the end of the day, Miss Lena's class was asked to join the other grade-six classes out in the assembly area. Peijing and Joanna sat in the back, their knees touching. Miss Sara was organizing a fundraiser for kids starving in an unprecedented famine in another country.

Everyone was going to take home a booklet that had twenty blank pages. They were to ask people they knew to write down their details and note how much they wanted to donate.

It was for a very urgent and immediate humanitarian cause because kids were starving in Africa. When Miss Sara spoke about it, she had tears in her eyes.

"Just as long as the kids don't come over here and speak their own language," Joanna whispered to Peijing.

"We're not supposed to be talking," replied Peijing, breaking the rule herself.

The spot where their knees touched made Peijing feel as if they were both profoundly connected and that it meant something to a universe that brought them together.

"It started to rain so much that the land became flooded," said Biju. She lovingly patted the boat she had been drawing, each plank of wood a different color. "But just like magic, the tiny boat the boy's grandmother had given him grew into a life-size one, and he climbed aboard.

"The first living thing he came across was a dog, almost exhausted from swimming. So he pulled the dog out of the water. The dog was very appreciative and licked his face."

"Do you think Ba Ba and Ma Ma would let us have a dog one day?" Peijing wondered aloud.

"The flood became as tall as the trees. The next thing the boy came across was a cat stuck at the top of one, arching as high as it could to keep itself from drowning. So he pulled the cat out. The cat purred in appreciation."

"Or if we can have a cat," said Peijing, as any sort of pet would be exciting. Their house had a lawn; they had room for a pet.

"The flood now covered even the tallest trees. The boy came across a swarm of bees, so tired from flying that their wings were giving up. So he let them on the boat. They built a hive and gave him honey.

"But still the boy's grandmother's warning loomed. Rescue all the animals. Don't rescue any humans."

CHAPTER FOURTEEN

Can I please have some donations for my book? It's for an urgent and immediate humanitarian cause," Peijing said at the dinner table.

"Can someone please pass me the rice?" asked Ba Ba.

"Who are you again, child?" asked Ah Ma to Peijing.

"I am your favorite grandchild," Biju replied for Peijing.

The good news was that, just as Peijing predicted, Biju had completely forgotten about yesterday's forks-and-spoons debacle. She was sitting there happily eating her meal with her chopsticks, her little legs kicking under the table—as Biju's energetic lower half was apt to do, even when the rest of her body had come to a standstill.

The bad news was that Ma Ma was angry.

She had stood across the road from the school when she came to pick Peijing up, so that in a moment of dread Peijing had thought Ma Ma had not come for her at all. She had forbidden her daughters to have secret time in their room when they got home. Peijing was to start straightaway on her homework and Biju was to practice her letters and numbers, while Ma Ma angrily mopped the pink floor tiles.

"What am I going to do if I am not allowed to bring lunch to my daughters?" muttered Ma Ma now, ignoring everyone at the table.

"You can always make me a sandwich like everyone else," replied Peijing.

Ma Ma looked at her with a horrified expression. It was also full of hurt. "You're not a Westerner, Peijing. You're Chinese."

"What's wrong with being a Westerner?" Peijing found herself replying. It was later that she realized she had yet to master this new superpower of free speech. "If you don't want us to be Westerners, why did you bring us to a Western country?"

"Peijing!" said Ma Ma, her voice rising. "You leave the family table right this instant!"

Horrified, Peijing stood up immediately. She hadn't meant to offend Ma Ma. The words had just come out of her, spilling out of her mouth like a tidal wave.

"I want to be a Westerner," said Biju out of the blue.

"Biju, you leave the table as well," said Ma Ma.

Pejing looked over at Biju, but Biju was full of defiance. Her little sister made a big show of chewing the food in her mouth, and only after had she swallowed it all did she hop down from her chair.

Ba Ba sat at the table and watched, but he didn't say anything.

Ah Ma sat with a blank look on her face and her chopsticks still in her hand. After a while, she started eating again.

Pejing and Biju scattered away down the hallway and hid themselves around the corner, patiently waiting for everyone to finish dinner.

They watched as Ba Ba came out of the dining room first and headed toward his study. He was followed by Ah Ma, who went to the living room. Finally, Ma Ma came out and stood in the hallway with her hands in her hair. Ma Ma did the only thing she had control of, and that was taking care of the shininess of the pink tiled floor. She got out the mop and bucket, and she started cleaning. Even though the pink floor tiles were already clean.

Peijing tried to remember if Ma Ma mopped the floor every day back at their old home, and she couldn't remember Ma Ma doing so. She remembered instead a mooncake sliced into quarters, the yolk suspended in the middle like the full moon, and sparklers dancing in the dark. She forced herself to look back at the real world. It loomed much too realistic, much too close.

"Let's go," said Peijing, touching Biju on the shoulder. The two girls disappeared silently into the safety of their own bedroom. Peijing closed the door, took out the Little World.

Biju was on a mission to draw bees. She said she was going to draw a hundred of them as a world without any meant no apples, plums, persimmons or bitter melon, although she didn't mind too much about the bitter melon.

Peijing came to join her little sister and helped her draw her bees. Uncharacteristically, Peijing drew one with a tiny black cat's face and wondered if anyone would notice.

"Can I call you Bee-ju?" asked Peijing. It was not often she made a joke.

"Yes," said Biju, completely missing the joke because her sister didn't often make jokes. Peijing didn't mind because she wasn't feeling that cheerful anyway.

After they had both immersed themselves and drank their fill of their world, they both lay down on their beds and stared up at the ceiling. Biju between her two giant bolsters, Peijing on her empty bed, the princess phone next to her, still unconnected.

The ceiling was a fresh white square atop the pale pink walls. It was new, like everything else in the house, and perfect.

"It's audition day tomorrow," said Biju. "Wait till Ma Ma sees me on the stage as a beautiful princess. When the curtain goes down at the end, people will throw roses for me. Ma Ma will be sorry she spoke to me in that voice."

"That's good," Peijing said.

Peijing did not have the heart to say in that moment that she was sure Ma Ma would not come. She looked at the smile on her sister's face and wanted desperately for her to stay in her own happy little world for as long as possible. Out there, Peijing could not protect her.

And she desperately wanted to protect her sister from Ma Ma mopping the pink floor tiles over and over again. From Ba Ba's indifference. From Ah Ma just sitting there as if she didn't know what was happening.

"Do you ever wonder why there are no people in the Little World?" Biju asked.

On any other day, Peijing would have replied with, "I don't know."

But on this occasion, she found herself instead saying, "It's because humans are too complicated."

"Do you mean to draw?" asked Biju. "Is this about those cauliflower hands silly Mrs. Jiang told you about once?"

Peijing did not answer. Just made Biju brush her teeth and change into her pajamas.

"With his new animal friends, the boy journeyed along in his boat. It had now rained for one hundred days straight. The flood was as high as the tallest mountain. That was when the boy saw a man clinging to life on the last remaining peak," said Biju.

"He remembered his grandmother's words. 'Rescue all the animals. Don't rescue any humans.'"

"'Help!' called out the man.

"The boy thought of his grandmother's words again, but because he was softhearted, and he felt sorry for the man, pulled him off the peak, and allowed him onto the boat.

"That was his mistake. The man saw that the boat had a lion's-head mast and that the lion's head was embedded with two real pearls for eyes. When the boy and the animals were sleeping that night, the man rocked the boat, so they all fell into the water. Then he sailed off, taking the boat and those pearls for his own."

"Is that the end of the story?" said Peijing incredulously.

"Yes," said Biju. "The moral is not to trust people."

"You're right, Ma Ma's stories really are a bit . . ." Peijing's mouth pulled into a sad frown, unsure about the words to describe this adult lesson.

CHAPTER FIFTEEN

Today, Peijing's backpack was a little heavier. Sitting inside was her old insulated lunch box, the compartments filled with rice, vegetables, and an oyster sauce omelette. She had found it sitting on the kitchen bench, and, even though Ma Ma did not say anything about it, had not even acknowledged its existence, Peijing knew that it meant Ma Ma would not be visiting the school in the afternoon.

In the car, Peijing tried to figure out if the days that Ma Ma had come to the school with a hot lunch for her were happy days, if she would indeed look back at them when she was grown and feel her heart grow warm. She wasn't sure. All she knew was that sometimes things came and were gone faster than she could build memories from them, and that scared her. Her stomach tensed. Full of snakes.

"I'm going to blitz my audition, just you all wait

and see," said Biju from the back seat. "I will not want to know you all when I am rich and famous."

Ba Ba was busy looking at his watch.

Ba Ba did not ask, "What audition?"

Peijing looked for Joanna as soon as she stepped into class. She found the girl facedown on the desk, her forehead pressed against her folded hands. She sat down and tapped Joanna's shoulder gently.

"Daddy, I promise I haven't fallen asleep! I'll make dinner straightaway!" Joanna exclaimed and sat up straight. "Oh, it's you, Peijing. . . . Well, thank goodness for that!"

Joanna smiled at Peijing as if she was part of a good dream.

"Here, have this," said Peijing. She reached into her backpack for the one thing she had been trying to carry very carefully all the way to school. She placed the package on the desk and unwrapped the paper napkin to reveal a steamed red bean bun.

Peijing had snuck it away from the breakfast table this morning. She had felt rebellious, but also very righteous about it. Among all the things she quietly worried about, this felt like a good and solid thing she could do something about. The bun was now cold, and the paper on the bottom had shrunk and stuck on tightly, but it was still perfectly okay to eat.

Joanna picked it up without question and crammed the whole thing in her mouth. Peijing had to make her take it out to remove the paper first. She could see the hunger in the girl's eyes, shining bright on the film of tears in her eyes.

"It's good," Joanna said, after she had swallowed and licked her lips.

"Hi," said a voice that made them jump out of their secret world.

Gemma Snowshoe cleared her throat. She was a vibrant and loud thing, a head taller than both of them. Peijing remembered marveling when Miss Lena had introduced her. Gem. It had made her think of diamonds and precious things. Gem held on tightly to a large stack of pink envelopes.

"Normally, I would never invite just anybody to my birthday party," she said.

Peijing looked eagerly at the envelopes in Gem's hand. Maybe she was being selfish, but she missed going to birthday parties. Back at her old school, she was popular and had lots of friends and was always invited to parties.

But at this school the rules had changed, and she was somewhere near the bottom, if not actually at the bottom. And it had happened like that overnight.

It was circumstance. Peijing didn't know if you could fight circumstance. She looked over to Joanna. There was a piece of hair stuck to the girl's lip with drool.

Peijing wondered what her old friends would think about this. They wouldn't believe it. She didn't know if she did herself.

"Daddy is paying a lot of money organizing an alpaca petting farm," explained Gem. "As I need to make up the numbers, I am making exceptions." Gem handed Peijing and Joanna an invite each. Peijing looked at the pink envelope in surprise. It was a small miracle.

"Are these real alpacas?" said Joanna, narrowing her eyes and acting like she got invited to birthday parties every weekend. "If it ends up being two men inside a suit, I won't be very impressed."

"There will be three alpacas. One of each color," said Gem, and she smiled proudly. "I will only let some people hand-feed them carrots."

"We will think about it," said Joanna. "No promises." She stared at Gem until Gem looked nervously away and moved off to the next group of kids who hopefully would be more thankful for their invites.

Peijing ripped open her envelope excitedly and looked at the invitation inside. It had an illustration of three alpacas, black, brown, and white, dancing around the border. She wondered if that was what would be at the party, or if it this was one of those situations where you expect one thing and end up being let down.

"Gem is a show-off, that's all," said Joanna. She did not open her envelope.

"But it's an invitation, anyway," said Peijing. "Aren't you excited to go?"

Joanna did not answer.

"You are not going," said Ma Ma at the dinner table.

Peijing looked dumbfounded at Ma Ma. She went to parties all the time. Ma Ma loved to put her in that blue satin party dress and tie her hair in two pigtails on either side of her head.

"It's a classmate's birthday," Peijing repeated, in case Ma Ma had not heard correctly.

"We don't know who this girl is. Everyone is a stranger, and it's not safe to go to strangers' homes."

"Maybe if you become friend's with Gem's mother, then she won't be a stranger anymore."

Ma Ma stared at Peijing as if her daughter had just asked to wear shoes inside the house or take a sandwich for lunch or use a fork or spoon.

"Do you think I can become friends with her by

speaking English?" Ma Ma pinched the bridge of her nose and looked down at the table. She said her head hurt.

Peijing didn't dare press the issue further. Instead, she turned inward and thought about the alpacas. In her imagination, they galloped around on rainbows and clouds, but that didn't matter 'cos there were no alpacas for her. She felt dreadfully sorry for herself.

She did not understand why Ma Ma would say that her classmates were all strangers; did she ever consider that maybe they—the Guo family—were actually the strangers? Peijing looked over to Biju to see if she could find an ally in her sister, but Biju was unusually quiet, an unmoving expression like a Peking opera mask glued to her face.

"Whose party are you going to? Is it my birthday party?" asked Ah Ma.

Peijing patted Ah Ma gently on the arm. "You aren't allowed to have birthdays anymore, remember?"

"Who are you again, child?" asked Ah Ma.

"I'm Peijing," she whispered in return.

Ah Ma seemed still confused. Peijing went quiet.

After dinner, Peijing sat on the couch with Ah Ma for a little while. She thought that maybe Ah Ma kept forgetting about her because she wasn't spending enough time with her. They didn't talk about anything, and Ah Ma seemed tired, but Peijing just wanted her grandmother to know she was there. The TV played the same news on endless repeat until Peijing didn't know what to do anymore, so she quietly left. Ah Ma watched the first news story as it looped back again and exclaimed in surprise to no one in particular.

Upon entering the bedroom, Peijing was greeted with the horrifying sight of Biju sitting on the pink carpet, the discarded pink envelope at her bare foot. Biju held her sister's invitation up to her face.

"Don't touch my things," said Peijing in a voice that came out bitterly.

"I want to go too," said Biju.

"No!" replied Peijing. "It's only for big kids," she added, even though Ma Ma had already told her she wasn't allowed to go at all.

"I don't care about a stupid party. Nobody cares about me!" Biju tossed the invitation to one side and hid her face in her arms.

"That's not true," said Peijing, softening.

"Well, if they did, then they would have given me the role of the princess, but they didn't!"

"Oh," said Peijing. This is what it was about. She

should be mad at Biju for caring about herself more than she cared about anyone else. But Biju was just a child. Maybe she was just as confused as Peijing was. With Ah Ma; with Ma Ma. With Ba Ba even. So many problems colliding together and falling out of the sky all at once.

She looked over at the hunched figure of Biju, which slowly swiveled itself to face away from her.

"Did you get any role?"

"Yes."

"That's great! What is it?"

"The sun," said Biju, staring at the wall. "It is the worst role ever! It isn't even a speaking part! They think my English is bad; that is what they are trying to say."

"I think the sun is important. We all need the sun."

Silence.

"And it's not true that nobody cares about you. I do."

"You're my sister—you don't count!" shouted Biju, and her shoulders started to heave. She walked over to her bed, retrieved one of her bolster pillows, and sobbed into it. Peijing watched with a lump in her throat, but she let her sister rage and cry. She tried not to take Biju's words of rejection to heart.

"I'm not beautiful enough to be a princess any-way," said Biju after all her tears had dried up and her eyes had swollen shut.

"I think the sun is more beautiful than any prin-cess," said Peijing. She knew she was trying to say the right words to comfort her sister, but when she really thought about them, it was not untrue. "What is your costume like?"

"I have to ask Ma Ma to find me a yellow outfit," replied Biju, hiccupping. "Mr. Brodie sprayed some raw spaghetti with gold paint. When it's dried, I will glue it onto a headband, and it will be my sunrays."

"Hang on," said Peijing. "You get to wear a crown? Why didn't you say so?"

"I do," said Biju thoughtfully and she bit her thumb. "The princess only gets to wear a silver crown. Mine is gold."

"Much better!"

"Silver is second place—gold is first place!" Biju couldn't help but start grinning.

Peijing grinned back.

"Thanks for being good to me," Biju said. "Some-times I think you and Ah Ma are the only two who care."

"It's okay. I just want to help," replied Peijing, and it was true. That's all she ever wanted. She touched her hand to Biju's hot face. In a way she was glad her sister was worried about school plays and spaghetti crowns. Small controllable things. Sweet, simple things.

LAST QUARTER
OF THE MOON

"The moon goddess is starting to look quite terrible now," said Biju. "She can hardly bear to show her face."

"When is the jade rabbit going to return to the moon to brew her more immortality potion?" asked Peijing.

"When I forgive her for cutting my ear," said Biju. "But till then, he's going to remain hidden. Even you can't find him."

CHAPTER SIXTEEN

Peijing woke up early the next morning, a mystery having kept her awake most of the night. She searched all the forests and meadows and fields of the Little World, all the places the rabbit might be. She even searched the Arctic sea, in case he was somewhere he ought not to be, but he was nowhere to be found. He was definitely not on the paper moon.

Ma Ma was sitting in the kitchen, still pinching the bridge of her brow between her fingers as if she hadn't moved from yesterday. She brought a packet of painkillers down from the top shelf and swallowed two with a mug of water.

Ma Ma touched her forehead and then touched her stomach. Peijing touched her stomach too. Snakes. For a fleeting moment, she felt as if they might both have the same problems, that they might both talk. Then Ma Ma was a whirlwind around the kitchen again, putting baos into the steamer and packing school lunches. Two mugs of three-in-one coffee mix. The moment passed.

"Peijing?"

"Huh?" Peijing turned to face Ba Ba with a sense of hope. Ba Ba looked strange wearing just a business shirt, chinos, and a windbreaker. Apparently, nobody at his work wore a suit and tie. Ba Ba had embraced this strange new custom and did not look unhappy for it. In fact, there was an even stranger custom called Free Dress Friday when you could go to work in a polo shirt and jeans.

"You can get out of the car now."

"Oh. Sorry," said Peijing. She realized she had been staring blankly out the window, the car had been parked for a while, and she had not recognized her school. She quickly got out.

"G'day," said Joanna as she appeared alongside Peijing, wheeling a huge rusty old bike.

"What a heap of junk," said an older boy as he walked past. "I know your dad is broke and drinks all your money away, but that is something from the Third World."

Joanna said nothing.

Peijing glared at the boy, realizing too late that he could actually see her expression.

"What are you staring at? Go back to China and starve if you think we're not good enough for you here."

Peijing's heart was beating fast. She wanted to yell at the boy to take back what he'd said about Joanna. She wanted to punch him in the face for saying what he had about her. Then she wanted to run out of the school gates, run until she reached the ocean, and, even though she could not swim, make it impossibly back home.

It wasn't until they were both together inside the magic tree that Peijing turned to Joanna and said, "I'm sorry about what happened at the bike rack."

"They do that all the time to me." Joanna shrugged. "I'm sorry they said you should go back to China when you're not even from China."

"Why would they pick on you?" Peijing asked. A long strand of blond hair had deposited itself on her knee. She let it remain there.

"People will always find something about you to pick on, if they want. You're never rich enough, pretty enough, smile enough, have the right parents, have the right possessions. I've stopped caring. So I just be myself."

Peijing thought about what sort of person she would be if she could be herself. She wanted to be that person brave enough to go running down the road screaming and turning into a billion atoms. But the weight of the world on her shoulders immobilized her.

"I like who you are," Peijing said to Joanna.

"I like the way you are too," said Joanna.

And in that moment, it felt like it was okay not to have everything worked out and not to be perfect.

Peijing waited by the gate after school, looking out for Ma Ma. She stood there patiently until all the other kids had gone and only a few loiterers were left kicking at each other. Then she became highly upset. Ma Ma wasn't coming.

She hurried quickly to the kindergarten. Biju was the only one left in her class, sitting by herself. Peijing apologized to Mr. Brodie.

"Is everything okay?" asked Mr. Brodie.

Peijing assured him that everything was fine, worried that the teacher would think Ma Ma was a bad mother when Ma Ma was not a bad mother. Really.

"Do you need me to call your mum?"

Peijing hastily shook her head and hurried Biju out of there.

"Where is Ma Ma? Why is she not here?" said Biju, her voice escalating.

"Ma Ma asked me to pick you up and take you home," Peijing lied. She would do anything to protect Ma Ma. Protect their family. Pretend everything was okay. It was the honorable way.

The two sisters walked home in silence. Biju was sucking her thumb. Peijing clutched her tummy uneasily. She honestly felt like crying. There would be a reason. Something simple and silly that would make all her anxiety rush away from her, and she'd wonder why she'd been so worried.

"G'day again," said Joanna as she appeared from a side street, wheeling her rusty old bike.

Peijing could not be happier to see anyone.

"I'll walk with you both," said Joanna. "You should ask your parents for a bike. We can ride together then, it's so much faster that way."

Peijing did not want to tell Joanna that today was just a one-off, that everything would be the same again tomorrow. Ma Ma would be walking them home like she always did.

"That is an adult's bike," said Biju, pulling her thumb out of her mouth. "In fact, that is a man's bike. There is no way you can ride on that."

"Course I can," replied Joanna. "In fact, I bet I can even dinky you."

"What does that mean?"

"I sit you on top of the handlebars and pedal both of us."

"That is ridiculous," said Biju.

Then, after a brief pause: "How do I get on?"

Joanna got Peijing to hold the bike steady while she helped lift Biju up. Biju promised she would hold on tight. Joanna jumped on the bike herself and the two of them went wobbling down the footpath for a short distance. Before they fell over onto the grass.

"My goodness! Are you both okay?" Peijing ran up and stared at them. Lying on their backs, they both gazed up at her slightly dazed.

"Oh, yuck! There is dog poop on the ground!"

That got Joanna and Biju quickly moving. By some divine act from a higher source or a very fortunate bit of chance, both of them had fallen toward the poop, but had landed in such a way that they avoided it. The three girls stared at the grass, then they stared up at the sky. Then they looked at one another and started howling in laughter.

Joanna picked up her bike and they continued walking, no talk of another dinky. But the buzz they all felt from a tragedy avoided opened up the universe, and they talked freely about other things, like school and weekends and whether any of them were old enough to like boys yet (of course not), and, for that distance of time, Peijing stopped feeling like she was full of other people's pain.

"Are you going straight ahead?" asked Joanna as they reached the break in the road. "This is where I have to turn."

"I'd like to ask you come to our house, but my mum won't like it," said Peijing.

"Well, I'd like to ask both of you over too," said Joanna hesitantly, "but I'm not sure if my dad would like it either."

Joanna did not explain why.

"But, if we catch him in one of his rare good moods, he might give me a few bucks so we can rent a video and get a jumbo popcorn."

Peijing thought that sounded like the best dream in the world, but Ma Ma said Joanna was a stranger, so Peijing said nothing. They stared at each other with moons in their eyes, careful not to sigh.

Biju misunderstood it for reality and started quizzing Joanna on what type of movie they would get and whether she would like popcorn, never having had popcorn before. Peijing tried to get Biju away, before Joanna started filling out details of this fantasy and made it more real for all of them.

Joanna, though, followed them up the road even though she was supposed to turn and talked about the video store, how it smelled like freshly buttered popcorn and had a whole aisle with all the kids' movies, both new releases and old classics, and broke Peijing's heart.

"I think you should go," said Peijing before Joanna could continue.

"Oh," said Joanna, and she stopped in her tracks. "I guess I'll see you tomorrow, then." She hastily reversed her bike, jumped on awkwardly, and rode away. She looked over her shoulder just the once, and Peijing wished she could call out to her to change her mind and stay.

Peijing sighed and walked the rest of the way with Biju in silence. Coming up the driveway and putting her hand on the handle, she knew something was wrong. The front door was unlocked. She entered cautiously; Biju barreled past her down the hallway.

Ma Ma suddenly appeared and caught Peijing by surprise. There was something wrong with Ma Ma; her face had turned as pale as the skin of a bao. She held her hands against her cheeks.

"Where's Ah Ma?" asked Peijing, suddenly aware that the couch in front of the TV was empty.

"She's gone! I went to have a shower, and when I came out, she was gone!"

"Do you remember the story about the boy and the boat?" asked Biju.

"The one with the awful ending? I don't want to think about it," replied Peijing.

"It turns out Ma Ma thought the story ended there, but it doesn't. I asked Ah Ma, and she said that after the bad man stole the boat, the boy's grandmother—who turned out to be a celestial being sent to test the world—caused the boat to shrink again. The bad man fell into the water and was never seen again."

"What happened to the boy?" asked Peijing breathlessly.

"The boat was returned to him, and he lived on it happily with his new animal friends, never lonely again," said Biju. She gave her sister two thumbs up.

"He didn't get into trouble with the celestial being for disobeying the rules and saving that human?" Peijing was very concerned about this.

"No," said Biju.

"So, in the end, kindness wins," said Peijing happily.

"Does it really, though?" asked Biju with a frown.

"Yes," replied Peijing firmly.

CHAPTER SEVENTEEN

Peijing could not understood why Ma Ma was just standing there. How long had she been standing there? How long had Ah Ma been gone?

"I always lock the front door with the key. When I came out of the bathroom, the door was wide open. . . ."

Peijing could not understood why Ma Ma wasn't doing anything.

And she hadn't explained why she didn't show for school pickup.

"We have to call the police," said Ma Ma and finally marched to the kitchen. There she took the receiver off the wall. And handed it to Peijing.

"What is happening?" said Biju, sticking her head in. "Where's Ah Ma?"

Peijing stared down at the receiver in confusion.

Then it dawned on her that Ma Ma expected her to make the call, because, of course, Ma Ma did not speak English.

At that moment, Peijing did not want to be an adult.

She was scared that Ah Ma was gone, she was scared to talk to the police, she was upset that it was all on her.

Peijing looked up at Ma Ma, and she seemed scared too. In the doorway, Biju started sucking her thumb again.

Ma Ma handed Peijing the special magnet on the fridge that had all the emergency numbers printed on it.

Peijing thought of all the movies and shows on TV with heroes in them. None of the heroes were ever eleven-year-old girls who couldn't even hold the receiver of the telephone properly because they were shaking so badly. She ran her finger down the magnet and found LOCAL POLICE STATION. She dialed the number.

"Hello, Summerlake Police Station, how can I help you?"

Peijing froze.

"Hello?"

"Hello." Her voice came out too loud.

The expectant faces of Ma Ma and Biju loomed toward her.

"How can I help you, sweetheart?"

"My Ah Ma . . . I mean my grandmother . . . has gone missing."

"Do you have an adult there with you, sweetheart?"

"I do. But my mother doesn't speak any English."

Peijing tried not to gulp in big mouthfuls of air.

"Listen carefully to me. You'll organize an interpreter for her, yes?"

"Yes," said Peijing.

"I will see you when you come down, okay?"

"Okay." Peijing hung up the phone. Her hand was still shaking.

"What did they say?" asked Ma Ma, leaning in closer.

Peijing felt like she couldn't breathe.

"We have to go down to the police station in person."

"We can't do anything until Ba Ba comes home, then," Ma Ma whispered, and she started putting her hands on her cheeks again.

"We can," said Peijing. "We will walk there. Biju, you can walk big distances, can't you?"

Biju nodded and stretched out one of her legs, as if to demonstrate how strong it was.

"I don't know how to read the road map. I don't know how to read the road signs." Ma Ma shook her head.

"I'll do my best to help," said Peijing, trying not to think about how bad she was at geography and her less-than-remarkable grade for it. "And we can ask directions along the way. People will help us."

"No," said Ma Ma and shook her head again. "No."

The word that Peijing was trying to find suddenly crystallized.

That word was "disappointment."

Disappointment with her mother.

When I grow up, I will not be like Ma Ma, Beijing thought in her head.

And no, I will not smack my mouth.

She took one last look at Ma Ma before she ran out the door.

As she felt the slam of the front door behind her, the echo of her own breathing as she ran from the veranda, the jarring of her knee on the driveway as her foot hit the concrete harder than she expected, Peijing's world became one of noise and confusion. As she ran toward the giant green park across the road, she felt as though she was seeing things less through her own eyes, but more through a shaky camera that lurched her body and stomach forward. Peijing ran until she stopped, heaving, at the park bench.

A man was walking his dogs, a couple held hands, the whole world out there carried on as normal, oblivious to what was happening inside of her. Peijing gulped down air and tried to calm herself. She sat down on the bench under that huge blue sky and stared up with weak eyes.

"Excuse me," she said to the man with the dogs. "How do I get to the police station from here?"

"Are you all right? It's quite a long distance from here," he replied, examining her closely.

When she didn't reply, but just stared back, he pointed across the park.

"If you head toward the school and keep going, you'll eventually come across it. It's on the same road, but at the opposite end. I wouldn't try to walk it if I were you."

The man went on his way with his dogs. A piece inside of Peijing wanted to shout, *Wait!* She wanted it to be like the movies, where a girl could befriend a man walking three dogs at once and they ended up helping each other. But the man soon became small on the horizon.

She looked back toward the direction of her

house, and two little figures appeared. They crossed the road, Ma Ma and Biju holding hands, and when they reached Peijing they stood opposite her like strangers.

Peijing turned away from them and marched across the park, calling Ah Ma's name. The world never seemed bigger or more intimidating, the sky so expansive and the ground so flat and wide. Peijing screamed Ah Ma's name until her throat became hoarse and dry. Her eyes prickled. Ma Ma and Biju followed behind, so small.

At the end of the park, Peijing looked in either direction. It would only make sense for Ah Ma to come out of the open front door, walk across the park, and then come to this exact spot where she stood right now. The right led to the school and, just beyond, a little group of shops. The left was only bushland.

Peijing did not like the bushes in Australia. When you walked past them, something unseen and mysterious always rustled inside. Peijing swallowed.

If Ma Ma had taken Ah Ma out more often instead of just letting her sit in front of the TV, Ah Ma wouldn't have tried to run away, Peijing thought angrily. But then she thought about the incident at the school supply store and how Ma Ma didn't like going out herself. That Ah Ma might not have much control over her actions and what she did anymore. Peijing rubbed her eyes and turned right.

Ma Ma and Biju caught up with Peijing, and she felt glad that they all walked side by side. She hated seeing Biju with nothing to say, sucking on her thumb even though she insisted she was not a baby anymore. Ma Ma in her baggy T-shirt and her hair in a rubber band that once held baby bok choy from the market back in Singapore. So different from the Ma Ma in her fashionable pink two-piece outfit from OG.

Peijing just wanted to find Ah Ma so that they could all go home.

They passed the school and then reached the corner store, painted with bright pink galah birds. Peijing looked inside, and, to her surprise, she saw Ah Ma standing among the aisles. She clapped her hands to her mouth. Peijing tore inside, not caring that the plastic straps across the doorway hit her in the face.

"Ah Ma, what are you doing here all alone?" Peijing composed herself, tried to act ordinary.

"I just went to the shop to buy some bread," said Ah Ma, as if it were something she did every day. "But then I realized I have no money, so I will have to go home and get it. Although, come to think of it . . . I am not sure how to get home."

"I will show you," said Peijing. She put her hand into the crook of Ah Ma's arm.

"Thank you, child. What did you say your name was again?"

"It's me, Peijing."

"Of course," replied Ah Ma and smiled.

And with that, Peijing burst into tears.

"There's no need to cry! Tell me what's wrong," said Ah Ma, patting her back. "Little girl, are you lost?"

Peijing led Ah Ma gently from the bread section and past the front counter. When she looked up at the shopkeeper, he spoke to her in his broken English.

"She has been here. Long time."

"I'm sorry," said Peijing, trying her hardest to explain. "She gets confused."

Biju had come into the store to stare at the candy and chocolates on display. Ma Ma was waiting outside with an angry expression on her face.

"I don't mind. She caused no trouble," said the shopkeeper, indicating toward Ah Ma.

"Can I have some candy?" Biju shouted to Ma Ma through the glass.

"No!" Ma Ma shouted back.

"Let's go," said Peijing, nudging her sister gently. She wanted to leave before she started crying again.

"Come over," said the shopkeeper.

Peijing approached the counter slowly, her arm still holding Ah Ma tightly.

The shopkeeper slid something across the counter. "Don't cry. For you. Be happy."

Peijing looked down at the counter. Sitting there was a small plastic package with a cartoon frog on the front. NOT FOR INDIVIDUAL SALE, read the words on the side. Peijing was so touched she grabbed the chocolate and pressed it into Biju's hand, shuffling all of them outside before she really did start to cry. They were far from the store before Peijing realized she hadn't thanked the shopkeeper.

Biju unwrapped the chocolate frog, broke the head off, and gave the rest to Peijing, who popped it into her mouth. It didn't taste like the chocolate back home, but it still tasted good. A tear rolled down her cheek. Biju ate the rest of the chocolate without saying anything; she probably did not remember what the chocolate tasted like back home.

Ma Ma's face became more and more angry as they walked. Peijing could see the words forming in her mother's pursed mouth as she stared at Ah Ma. *Why did you wander off like that? Do you know how much of a fright you gave me?* But Ma Ma remained silent.

The four of them headed home, like a strange, sad

creature with eight legs and a whole heap of emotions it couldn't control properly. Biju, who considered the Case of the Lost Ah Ma solved, wanted to talk about school and her upcoming play. Ah Ma would reply with things that made no sense, like, "Oh, look at those flowers, I wonder if they have a name," and, "When I was young, we used to make our own toys. We looped rubber bands together to make a skipping rope." Ma Ma still said nothing. Peijing said nothing either but, on the inside, felt everything.

"When Ba Ba comes home, I will ask him to get better locks for the door," said Peijing to Ma Ma, in the kindest voice she could muster. This was a thing she had learned to do. Instead of saying *I'm sorry* and *I forgive you*, because they were such a traditional family, she made gestures that meant the same thing in little actions

"I will let you go to that party," Ma Ma whispered. And by that she meant *I love you*. "But you must take your little sister with you."

Peijing wanted to bite down hard on her tongue. Everything was a never-ending cycle of getting mad, being glad, and then getting mad all over again. But she said nothing, just let everyone shuffle inside, then she levered the door handle up and down, testing it.

"This is a great test," Biju said solemnly as she unfolded a long river that reached from one end of the room to almost the other.

"What is?" asked Peijing.

Biju picked up a paper fish and held it up to Peijing's face.

"If this common carp can swim all the way up the Yellow River, it will face a raging waterfall at the very end. If it is brave enough to throw itself upstream and jump over the waterfall, a reward awaits."

"And that is?" asked Peijing.

"The gods will lift it up into the sky; it will grow legs and become a magnificent dragon with a place among the heavens for all of eternity."

From the doorway, Peijing could see Ma Ma bend over for no reason with her face in her hands.

"I think that is a foolish quest," snapped Peijing.

"Fine. Stay an ugly carp, then," snapped Biju. She folded the river back up roughly.

"I'm sorry," said Peijing.

"Not everyone can be a dragon," said Biju curtly, and that was that.

CHAPTER EIGHTEEN

Peijing guided Ah Ma toward the direction of her bedroom, next to Ma Ma and Ba Ba's room.

"Thank you for bringing me home, child. If you tell me who you are, then I can repay you."

"I'm still Peijing, and I love you, grandmother," said Peijing. She helped Ah Ma change into her comfortable floral pajamas and put her dentures into a glass of water. Spread cooling rice paste onto her face.

"Thank you, Peijing," said Ah Ma, her face white like the moon as she lay down in bed for a nap after her big adventure. "As the proverb goes: 'Man may be the head of the family, but it is the woman who turns the neck.'"

Peijing smiled sadly and affectionately patted the top of Ah Ma's covers.

When she went to find Biju after their grandmother fell asleep, her sister was in the middle of the bedroom floor, surrounded by savannas and subtropical grasslands. Their world was bountiful and overflowing. It made her think simultaneously how much she had and how much could be taken away from her.

Sitting out on the open grassland, wearing a miniature pair of paper sunglasses, was the jade rabbit.

"Isn't he supposed to be hiding from the goddess still?" asked Peijing as she sat down carefully on an uncovered patch of carpet.

"He's getting braver now, bold even," replied Biju, and did not elaborate any further.

A delicious four-dish dinner awaited the family like it always did at the end of the day. Ma Ma was still bringing food to the table, when Ba Ba, in his business shirt with no tie and chinos, showed Ma Ma an invite to a family picnic day that the company was organizing. Ma Ma asked if it was a formal gala. "No," said Ba Ba, "it's a picnic at the park." With a "BBQ," whatever that was. Ma Ma looked confused. Ba Ba wanted to chat and did not look like he was in a hurry to sit and wolf down his dinner in silence, like he usually did.

"I'm starving!" exclaimed Biju, who had barely

sat herself down when she reached over and snagged some chili snake beans with her chopsticks. Ba Ba cleared his throat, and Biju reluctantly placed the beans in Ah Ma's bowl instead. Ba Ba nodded at the correct course of action.

Ma Ma brought the big bowl of steamed rice to the table.

"Ba Ba, I want to get a bicycle," said Biju.

"Ba Ba, I think we need to look at getting a better lock on the front door," said Peijing, thinking of more sensible priorities.

"We can discuss this later," said Ba Ba.

"I want to go home," said Ma Ma and and started crying, still holding on to the bowl of rice.

Everyone turned to stare at Ma Ma in shock. The room went completely quiet.

Until it was suddenly filled with a strange noise.

At first Peijing thought Ah Ma was coughing, until she realized that Ah Ma was actually choking.

The room started moving very slow and really fast all at the same time. Ma Ma dropped the rice bowl in fright. It made a crack in the pink and perfect tiles and rolled away. Ba Ba flew over to Ah Ma and started thumping her back with a hard fist. Biju dropped her chopsticks.

Ah Ma made a few more strange noises, and suddenly something dislodged and came flying out. It was a piece of sweet-and-sour fish. Ma Ma's mouth was wide open. Ba Ba's white business shirt had come untucked.

"I'll go get the mop," said Ma Ma in shock.

Ah Ma started coughing uncontrollably. Peijing's parents looked at each other with concern.

"Don't worry about the mop," said Ba Ba.

"When I was a little girl, we used to loop rubber bands together to make a skipping rope," Ah Ma managed to say in between coughs. Ba Ba held tightly onto Ah Ma as if that would make things better.

Peijing was frozen. She could feel Biju just as stiff and unbreathing next to her.

"I think it's best both you girls go to your room," said Ba Ba.

"Everything is going to be okay," he said to Ma Ma.

"No, it's not," replied Ma Ma.

Under the table, Peijing felt Biju grip her hand tightly.

"Ma Ma and I are going to go straight to the hospital with Ah Ma, okay?" said Ba Ba. "Peijing, can I rely on you to look after Biju?"

Peijing nodded stiffly.

"You're a good girl," said Ba Ba.

Peijing nodded again, even though she was not sure those were the right words. She watched as Ba Ba put one of Ah Ma's arms over his shoulder and Ma Ma did the same on the other side. They helped guide her to the front door. Ah Ma hobbled weakly, even though she was not injured.

"Can you go to the bedroom?" Peijing whispered to Biju. "Maybe you can set out a little story for me? I'll be there shortly, okay?"

Biju nodded, her face drained of color, and she slipped away.

Biju was kneeling on the bedroom floor looking out the window. The moon, half of its usual self tonight, stood on its side as if it didn't know whether to be a smile or a frown. Peijing was surprised to find that no elaborate scene was set out waiting for her.

"I thought you were going to tell me a story?" she said.

"I am," said Biju. She took the paper rabbit from her palm and stuck it against the glass on the windowsill.

"The jade rabbit is going to return to the moon now. He can make the immortality potion again. I'm no longer angry with the moon goddess. I don't want her to die."

And with that, Biju burst into tears.

"There is something awfully wrong with Ah Ma, isn't there? She forgot how to swallow her food, didn't she? She forgets everything these days!"

Peijing wanted nothing more than to fuss over Biju and tell her that nothing was wrong with Ah Ma, that everything was going to be okay just like Ba Ba said.

"What do you think it is? Do you think it's cancer?"

"No, I don't think it's something like that!" exclaimed Peijing.

"What is it, then?"

"I'm not sure," said Peijing.

She held Biju while her sister cried herself into a hot and heavy sleep. Then she quietly padded out and down the hallway. The house was quiet. Ma Ma and Ba Ba were still not back. Peijing went to the kitchen with the mop and bucket and started cleaning up the spilled dinner on the floor, even though Ma Ma wouldn't like her helping because she couldn't do it properly. Then she curled up on the floor next to the phone.

From the light still on in the dining room across the hall, she could see the singular floor tile, cracked.

No matter how many times it would be cleaned over, it was never going to be perfect.

She must have fallen asleep at some point, as she woke up the next day in her bed, with no memory of anyone carrying her lovingly there and tucking her in.

"Once upon a time, the jade emperor organized a race for all the animals in the world," said Biju. "Only the first twelve crossing the finish line would be immortalized forever in the zodiac."

"The cheetah will win for sure," said Peijing. "It's the fastest animal on earth."

"No, the fastest would be the dragon," replied Biju.

"But dragons don't—don't worry, keep going."

"The first two to reach the river crossing were the rat and the ox, 'cos they are nice early risers."

"The ox started swimming across, and the rat said, 'Oh, can I please sit on your head? Look, I'm only small,' so the ox agreed. But as soon as they reached the other side, the rat jumped off and ran for the finish line. He came first! Oh, cheeky rat!"

"I'm not sure that is a great moral for a children's story," said Peijing with a frown.

"Little kids need to know how the world really works sooner or later," replied Biju and patted her sister on the shoulder.

CHAPTER NINETEEN

The morning brought with it the funny sight of Ba Ba sitting in front of the TV with his pajamas and slippers on, watching a morning news program. Peijing had never known her father to start the workday as casually as this. Biju saw it as a joke, and she tried to climb on him. Ba Ba grumbled and told her to be gentle, but he caught her before she fell to the ground on her head. The morning did not bring with it Ah Ma or Ma Ma.

"Where is everyone?' asked Peijing and threaded her fingers together.

"Ah Ma is going to be staying at the hospital for at least another night. Ma Ma is staying as well to keep an eye on her."

"I told you she has cancer!" said Biju in a tight voice, straightening up.

"Ah Ma does not have cancer," said Ba Ba, and

Biju went quiet. She sat with her knees together and sucked her thumb.

"What does Ah Ma . . . have?" asked Peijing quietly. People did not get admitted to hospitals for no reason, especially Chinese people, as hospitals were very unlucky and full of ghosts and you tried not to go if you could help it.

"Well," said Ba Ba, "they wanted to keep Ah Ma under surveillance as she was suffering from a mild case of shock after almost choking on her dinner. And she has a little bit of dehydration, so they've given her lots of fluids."

Peijing waited for the "but." She couldn't say how she knew exactly, but she had that feeling in her stomach again.

Ba Ba bowed his head and put his chin against his fists. He looked like he was having a very painful thought. Ba Ba was good at thinking about the big picture, at having grand visions about how communities and cities should be built to make large crowds of people happy—that was how they ended up in Australia. But Ba Ba was perhaps not so good when it came to thinking about individual members of his family. That had always been Ma Ma's job.

"Do you know how something can be invisible but still exist?"

Peijing immediately put her hand to her stomach. The snakes.

"Ah Ma has an illness. You can't see it, but you might have noticed that Ah Ma has had problems with her memory recently."

"Is it like the entire universe?" asked Biju.

"The entire universe?" echoed Ba Ba.

"No one knows the universe exists. They haven't even built a big enough telescope to see the edge of the universe. But it must exist. Because if it doesn't, then how are we here?" Biju said solemnly.

"I guess it's like that," said Ba Ba and scratched his head. Peijing swore she saw a piece of stardust, like a fast-moving miniature galaxy, fall out. She blinked and it was gone.

"So, it is important that we figure out a plan for Ah Ma," said Ba Ba quickly before he changed the subject.

"Do you want to know what the good news is? It means I'll be staying home for a few weeks to help look after Ah Ma and to help Ma Ma out. I'm going to take you both to school today and then pick you up, how about that?"

"Yay!" shouted Biju.

"Are you going to get changed?" asked Peijing. Ba Ba was wearing an old sleeping T-shirt, one he had gotten from a conference that read TRUST ME. I'M GOOD AT MAKING CONCRETE PLANS, a joke nobody understood, it seemed, except Ba Ba himself.

"I don't get out of the car," said Ba Ba. "Anyway, I don't think I care. We're in Australia now! I'm thinking the Australian way: that life is too short to worry about what other people think."

Peijing's eyes went big. Was Ba Ba still the same person from yesterday and all the days before? Ba Ba cared dreadfully about what other people thought. That's why his business suit always had to be perfect and why he worked so many extra hours so people would be impressed. But this Ba Ba grinned back at her.

She worried that Ba Ba's words were a terrible lesson to teach someone as impressionable as Biju, but her sister was too busy being tipped upside down by Ba Ba.

Peijing wondered what was going to happen to all of them. Ma Ma had always been the one to take care of them all, cooking and cleaning and sewing back on the buttons that Biju would chronically lose. Ah Ma was always there to answer all their difficult questions that they couldn't ask anyone else. How was Ba Ba going to fulfil any of these roles as well as being himself?

In the kitchen, Peijing lifted the lids of the leftovers in the fridge to try to put together a lunch. She packed her own schoolbag, packed Biju's schoolbag, and remembered it was library book return day. She moaned at Biju to brush her teeth and to get changed. Biju showed Ba Ba a loose button on her school shirt, and Ba Ba was not sure what to do about it.

Out on the driveway, Ba Ba stared intently at the car.

"It's such a nice day—why don't we all walk to the school instead?" he said. "Which way does Ma Ma take?"

Peijing pointed to the park with the impossibly blue sky. It hurt her eyes.

Biju thought it was a hoot to have Ba Ba there to show off in front of. She ran headfirst against the sky, daring to push it away. Peijing walked slowly, wondering if she was now upside down and the sky was actually water and she had not been told to swim.

Nobody seemed like the same person they were before they came to Australia. Not even Peijing. She was trying to hold on so tight to the person she used to be, but it seemed like the current of life was pushing her into new terrain, new places. She felt herself being helplessly shaped like a little stone tossed upon the shore.

"Ba Ba! Look at me!" called Biju, climbing up toward the monkey bars.

She made her way determinedly across and jumped down on the other side.

"Ta-da!" said Biju, as if performing the wold's greatest trick.

Ba Ba laughed and clapped his hands.

Peijing was surprised as she had only ever seen her father clap his hands once, and that was after the prime minister's very serious speech during the last Singapore National Day celebration.

The button had come clean off Biju's shirt and was now missing.

As her sister with her ever-listening ears skipped on ahead, Peijing seized the opportunity.

"Ba Ba, are you scared?" Peijing whispered, trying to keep it a secret from the rest of the world.

"I'm very scared," replied Ba Ba.

Peijing didn't know what to think. If Ba Ba, who was the head of the family, was only human, what did it mean for all of them?

"But we will do the best for Ah Ma, I promise you."

Peijing thought about what Ah Ma said, about the man being the head, but the women turning the neck. She wondered what it was the three of them—her, Biju, and Ma Ma—could do for Ah Ma.

Biju came running back, and Ba Ba filled his lungs with the cold morning air. He breathed out white clouds and pretended he was a dragon. Biju did the same, and they both howled with laughter. Ba Ba stopped to ruffle up a friendly dog and call him a good boy.

"Don't worry," added Ba Ba. "You are too young to have any worries."

Peijing worried about the sky.

"After the rat and the ox crossed the line, there were still ten places that needed to be decided in the race," said Biju.

"The monkey and the rooster both reached the river, but were sad because they were small and didn't know how to cross it. The sheep caught up and was going to float across like a big sponge. The sheep can do that 'cos she's made of wool."

Peijing wasn't convinced this was how the physics of sheep worked.

"But she was really kind. Listen to this next bit—you'll really like it because it's sensible."

Peijing declined to comment.

"Even though the sheep had heard what the rat had done, she still let the monkey and rooster ride across on her back. When they reached the other side, the other two said it was only right for the sheep to cross the finish line before they did."

"That story makes me feel better about the world," said Peijing, and she smiled.

"It takes all sorts for the world to go around," said Biju in all seriousness.

CHAPTER TWENTY

Are you both coming to my birthday party or not?" asked Gem with her hands on her hips. "I can only have the alpaca petting farm if I get the numbers. Plus, I have to know how many cupcakes and juice packs and sausage rolls to cater. It's a hard business organizing a party."

"I'm coming," said Peijing. She went to add that she had to bring her little sister as well, but then she started to panic. What if Gem said she couldn't go if she planned on bringing Biju?

Beside her, Joanna shuffled nervously on the spot.

"Yes," she finally said.

"Good," said Gem, and she moved onto the next group of kids.

"What's wrong?" Peijing asked Joanna. She wished that Joanna would in turn ask what was wrong with her. She shuffled nervously on the spot too.

"Dad says I can go to the party, but he says there is no money to buy a present. I don't know if I can go to a party without a present." Joanna looked at the ground.

"That's okay," said Peijing. "You can share my present."

"Really?" Joanna's face lit up.

"Of course. I'll write both our names on it."

And Biju's. But she would keep that quiet right now.

"You do realize I won't be able to pay you back for it? Maybe ever?" said Joanna.

"That's okay. Don't worry about it."

Joanna smiled, and the worry disappeared off her face.

Peijing smiled back. She felt sad, but also glad that her small actions could make such a difference. She thought about how Ma Ma and Ba Ba had thought it was her duty to always behave honorably and, right then, Peijing felt as powerful as an ancient warrior like Hua Mulan.

Twice a week, Miss Lena would lead her class to the lunch area, and there, upon the concrete stage, she would shed her ordinary teacher's blouse and pants to reveal, like a superhero, a shiny blue leotard with hot pink leggings underneath. She would play the latest pop hits out of her boom box, and everyone would do aerobics for half an hour.

Peijing and Joanna would stand at the back and concentrate very hard to follow her moves. From their vantage point, Miss Lena looked like a neon dream; she moved so fast that her arms became rainbow blurs. Sometimes Miss Lena would wear a matching headband to keep the sweat off her forehead.

Today the stage was still occupied by the kinder-gartners rehearsing their play. The king stood crying in the corner. The knight and the princess at center stage had decided they did not want to ride off together into the sunset after all. A group of hand-maidens looked around nervously, and hidden away in the back left-hand corner stood a dejected sun with a frown on her face.

"Let's start from the beginning of the play once again!" directed Mr. Brodie, wiping his brow. "And action!"

As per the script, Biju was supposed to rise resplendently from her corner. Instead, Biju jerked up abruptly, still frowning. While the scene in the king's court played out, Biju was meant to move sideways across the stage, judging it perfectly so she would reach the other side just in time to set upon a happily ever after.

Biju, though, rushed through it and had already reached her final destination before the play was even halfway through. Crossing her arms and glaring at everyone else, she tuned out completely, so that when it came time for her grand sunset moment, she completely missed her cue.

"How is it going?" Miss Lena asked Mr. Brodie.

"You know how it is, working with five-year-olds," Mr. Brodie replied. He wiped his brow again as he comforted the crying king. "It's like herding cats!"

Miss Lena nodded sympathetically.

Upon seeing Peijing, Biju leapt off the stage and barreled straight toward her sister, planting her face right into Peijing's shirt.

"IsastoopidpartandIdonwannadoit," she said.

"What did you say?"

Biju took a step back. "I said—it's a stupid part and I don't want to do it!"

"Do you know what I think?" replied Peijing, squatting down to look Biju in the eye. "I think the sun is the most important role because the play would not be able to begin if the sun did not rise."

"Hmmm," said Biju and sucked her thumb. "I guess."

"And it's the only role in the entire play that is on the stage the whole time!"

Biju took her thumb away. Wiped it on the back of her shirt.

"I've got an idea," said Peijing. "How about when you rise, you put your arms out wide and give a great big stretch? And when you reach the other side you give a yawn before you set? And most important, I think you should smile on the world as you move slowly across the stage. Like the real sun."

Peijing could see that Biju was thinking. Whenever Biju went without talking for a long time, it meant she was considering something very seriously. Squeezing Peijing just the once, she ran back up on the stage and there she stood, back in her corner, until Mr. Brodie again called, "Action!" and Biju rose up with conviction.

Peijing watched her with tears in her eyes. The pressure that remained around her neck from Biju's squeeze hung on her like a medal on a ribbon. Her throat felt tight. Biju looked so little yet so brave up on the stage. Peijing felt proud not only as the big sister, but also as the father, mother, and grandmother that she knew she had to be as well. Everything sad and everything happy made her want to cry these days. Everything was a feeling, a tiny universe under an immense pressure, keenly felt.

"I wish I had a little sister," said Joanna, sighing.

"You don't want this little sister, believe me," said Peijing, standing up and trying to brush it off. She shook her head and smiled and laughed, and her nose threatened to run.

Mr. Brodie gathered all his students together in rows of two, and Miss Lena took to the stage, shed her outer layers, and became Aerobic Woman. As the first song blasted out of the boom box and Miss Lena started marching her legs and pumping her arms above her head, the five-year-olds stared at her in amazement. Peijing followed the moves and felt, for the first time in a while, a sense of resolution and optimism.

"Guess which animal came twelfth—last!—in the zodiac contest?" asked Biju.

"I have no idea," said Peijing. She knew better than to try suggesting the slowest animal on earth as that would probably be the wrong answer.

"It was the pig!" exclaimed Biju. "Because she got hungry and stopped to have a snack!"

"I know someone born in the year of the pig," said Peijing affectionately. "And it would be very typical of them to stop for a snack."

Biju chuckled at herself.

Peijing couldn't help but remember that somewhere in the story a snake slithered underneath the feet of all the animals and crossed the finish line too. She put her hand on her stomach.

CHAPTER TWENTY-ONE

B a Ba was waiting for Peijing at the school gates after school, holding Biju's hand.

"The exercise this morning has given me a great enthusiasm," said Ba Ba. "I thought I would do it again."

Peijing was surprised that Ba Ba hadn't pulled a muscle as he hadn't been known to walk so much. He didn't even own a pair of sneakers, only five pairs of business shoes, all brown. He was wearing his flip-flops.

"Are you sure you're okay?" asked Peijing.

"Strong as an ox," said Ba Ba, thumping his chest.

Biju did a run-up and tried to climb onto his back.

"An old ox," clarified Ba Ba as he doubled over, but grinned happily.

Walking home, Peijing stared at Biju and wondered if she had behaved this freely and openly with her affections when she was that age. She couldn't remember; she couldn't imagine it.

All she knew was that when she was five, she had always been told to be a good girl and to stand up straight and mind her manners. Now she felt that, given permission to be who she wanted, it was much too late for her. That she was going to become an adult who worried about standing up straight and minding her manners and held everything on the inside.

At home, Peijing took the crumpled competition leaflet out of her schoolbag and tacked it onto the wall next to her bed. She stared at it and wondered whether, if she won the competition or even came runner-up, it would change her world.

Ma Ma and Ah Ma returned back home just before dinnertime. They had only been gone one night, but Peijing was sure that she had not seen them for longer because they both looked so small. Like how things such as chocolate bars, cream crackers, and bags of potato chips always seemed smaller the more time passed. Ma Ma's shoulders were slumped forward. Ah Ma looked an inch shorter.

Biju went up to Ma Ma and planted her face into her side. Peijing wanted to do the same thing to Ah Ma but resisted. Ma Ma did not try to move Biju away.

"Let Ma Ma and Ah Ma get some rest now," said Ba Ba.

He guided both of them toward their bedrooms and shut the doors.

For the first time ever, Ba Ba was cooking in the kitchen. Peijing hadn't even known Ba Ba could cook. Ba Ba said that during his bachelor days he used to live in a flat with three other men and he cooked all the time. Peijing did not know if he was joking.

"Dinner is ready!" called Ba Ba. He banged the saucepan with the wooden spoon.

Ba Ba had made a Western dish he said one of his old roommates had taught him how to make, but he failed to mention which part of the West it came from. He served the red sauce on top of boiled pasta and called it Bolognese, but it also had green peas, curry powder, and a chili in it. He gave everyone a plate along with a knife and a fork.

Biju picked up the fork without any sense of irony; she had forgotten all about the time she had tried to use a fork at the table. Peijing picked up the fork and she couldn't help but smile to herself.

Ba Ba tucked heartily into his own creation. Ma Ma had a few mouthfuls and then pushed it away quietly. Ah Ma looked at it confused, but then ended up eating the whole thing.

Peijing and Biju? They loved it! It was a novelty to eat something that was not Chinese food! Peijing mopped up all the sauce on her plate, and so did Biju, who actually licked the plate and made Ba Ba laugh. Peijing turned to Ma Ma, expecting Ma Ma to tell Biju off, but Ma Ma just gave a small smile.

Ba Ba set to work washing up after dinner, and Peijing asked if she could help.

"Why not?" said Ba Ba.

Peijing squirted detergent on the sponge and scrubbed a plate. The evening felt sad, but open in a way it hadn't for a long time.

She desperately wanted to ask Ba Ba about getting a bike. She wanted to know if she could deliver the local newspaper like some of the other kids did, or help around the house for pocket money, so she could save up to buy that bike.

And one day, when she was old enough, she was going to get a proper after-school job, and she was going to buy a car. She was going to drive away toward that prestigious art school of her dreams and never come back.

Even though she knew that, when she grew up,

she had the responsibility to care for both her parents and Ah Ma in their old age as she was the eldest. Even though she was also in charge of always keeping an eye on Biju and making sure she didn't make bad and strange choices in life.

She was going to do both things but didn't know how it could be accomplished without splitting herself in two.

"I know I can count on you," said Ba Ba.

Ba Ba had never stopped working long enough to look at the big, wide world, let alone to be interested in a Little World. But after the dishes were all washed and the surfaces wiped down, Ba Ba sat down at the dining table with Ah Ma and Ma Ma instead of going straight to his study, and something shifted. It shifted once again when Biju ran into the bedroom and came back out with the 24 X 200G ARNOTT'S TIM TAMS cardboard box.

Peijing froze. She instantly thought about the populations lost when humans had discovered animals previously hidden. The dodo. The Tasmanian tiger. Steller's sea cow.

But then she thought about conservation efforts

that had brought species back from the brink and that humans could be taught to care. The giant panda. The Blue whale. Trumpeter's swan.

It was hard to say. She felt she understood animals; felt she knew nothing about humans.

Ba Ba watched Peijing cut out a black sheep from paper.

It made Peijing incredibly nervous. She suddenly felt as if she had to cut that sheep out better than she normally did, so she ended up slicing it in half instead. Biju snickered and made a snide comment.

"What is wrong with it?" Ah Ma asked, confused. Ah Ma examined the back half of the sheep with great interest. She passed it to Ma Ma who took the two pieces and joined them back together again. Peijing watched how Ma Ma placed the sheep back down on the table and gave it a gentle pat.

"What do you call this . . . craft?" asked Ba Ba.

Peijing gently took out the red barn from the box and showed him how all the larger animals like the cows and horses fit at the bottom, how the chickens lived in the rafters.

"Interesting," said Ba Ba.

Peijing looked at him out of the corner of her eye, unsure whether to trust him.

• • •

As the house became quiet and the night settled in, Peijing once again found herself sitting alone next to Ah Ma on the couch.

"Did you have a good day today, Peijing?" asked Ah Ma.

Peijing turned in surprise. "You know my name."

"Of course I do," replied Ah Ma, raising an eyebrow. "I have two granddaughters who are my most favorite, and you are one of them. Mind you, I only have two granddaughters."

Ah Ma smiled, revealing her full set of dentures, and Peijing smiled too. The magic of the Mid-Autumn Festival came back to her. Peijing sniffed and dabbed her nose and swore she could see little gold glimmers from her cousins' sparklers falling down around them.

"Can I ask you a question, Ah Ma?"

"What is it?"

"What does it mean when you feel too much? Like you can't help it. You feel everything. And it really hurts your heart."

Peijing still worried about the lady that answered the phone at the police station. She worried about how she felt when no one showed up in person to make that missing person's report. She worried about the interpreter that was asked to come in. Peijing worried for complete strangers.

"Well," said Ah Ma, "I'm afraid I can't offer you much but the following proverb: You cannot prevent the bird of sorrow flying over your head, but you can prevent it building a nest in your hair. My own mother used to tell me that one."

It seemed that although Ah Ma would forget about today and yesterday, she was looking deep into Peijing's eyes and remembering something far more important.

Peijing smiled and the world sparkled a little brighter.

"You just have to let the feelings guide you, Peijing," said Ah Ma. "You will never be wrong if you are true to yourself. The world—your parents included—will always tell you to be the best version of yourself. I think that is wrong! What we all should be is our *favorite* versions of ourselves."

Ah Ma patted Peijing on the leg. "Now, do you have any more questions for me? You'd better ask them now, before your Ba Ba decides to take me away to a special home."

"Special home?" Peijing repeated. But as soon as she spoke the words, the magic was broken. Ah Ma's eyes became glued back to the TV screen. She held on to Ah Ma's hand even though it had become limp and heavy.

"Tell me a bedtime story," said Biju, barging in and landing heavily on Ah Ma's lap.

"Hello, child, I'm going to a special home!" said Ah Ma.

"What special home?" asked Biju.

"Somewhere safe, where no one will ever be able to find me," said Ah Ma.

"What is she talking about?" Biju said to Peijing.

Peijing had no idea. Being pulled away from her home with them and put somewhere else did not sound special; it sounded like a punishment. And Ah Ma had done nothing wrong.

"The rabbit?" exclaimed Ah Ma and gripped tightly onto Peijing's hand. "The moon! Don't forget about the rabbit! You must save the rabbit!"

Biju slid off Ah Ma's lap in fright and hung on to Peijing's arm.

"What is wrong with me?" Biju said, sitting up in the middle of the night. "My right leg hurts, like it's stretching from the inside."

Peijing got up and went to sit beside her sister.

"Nothing. You're just growing up. Sometimes that can hurt," said Peijing, and she wrapped her arms around Biju.

"What is the special home Ah Ma talked about?" Biju asked, her voice escalating.

"I think it's got something to do with Ah Ma's invisible illness." Peijing wanted to say something to make things better, to soothe it over like she always did. But she did not want to take the truth from Biju. She decided she was going to do this a lot more now.

The cold seemed to come right through the glass of the window, and even under three layers of blankets she could not feel warm some nights. So Peijing just gripped on tightly as she let her sister cry.

"I wish we could see everything that was invisible." Biju sniffed. Blew a snot bubble through one nostril.

"Well," replied Peijing, "imagine if we could see gravity, electromagnetic waves, black holes, the stars and moons all at once and all the time. It would be a bit much."

"I would like to see the stars all the time," said Biju with a whine.

"You'll see the stars when it's time for the stars," said Peijing. "Now it's time to see the insides of your eyelids."

She made Biju shuffle over on the single bed, and she cuddled up next to her. She thought it would take ages for them to fall asleep, that it would be hard. But to her surprise, it wasn't at all.

In her dreams, she saw a mooncake and a golden egg yolk and also the thought that had crossed her mind fleetingly and then disappeared into the night: that adults told kids to do one thing and then did another. It was not an honorable act to put Ah Ma into a special home.

Peijing slipped a little toward that pit of snakes, but she put out her arms and her legs and held on strongly to the sides of that pit like a warrior, so she wouldn't slip any further down.

"What about this little animal?" said Ba Ba, holding up the jade rabbit.

"The rabbit almost drowned trying to swim across by himself," said Biju in a practical voice. "But he managed to pull himself out of the currents and onto a log. There was a sudden gush of wind and he rode the log like a surfboard to the other side."

"Hold on," interrupted Peijing, "I thought the jade rabbit belonged to a different story?"

"Well," said Biju, thinking about it, "in a way we all belong to more than one story."

CHAPTER TWENTY-TWO

Peijing noted that everyone in Australia dressed very casually. Joanna had spoken about the one good outfit in her wardrobe that she was going to wear to Gem's party, the one her grandmother had bought her—an oversize purple blouse and denim dungarees. She was going to wear her hair tied to one side of her head with a scrunchie—like the girls in the teen magazines did.

The two matching satin dresses sitting side by side on Peijing's bed were definitely not something that would be seen in a teen magazine. It seemed like an eternity ago that Peijing had worn one dress (and Biju the other) to board the plane to come here. The girl who had worn that dress was now a stranger to her.

Peijing stuck her head in the wardrobe and took out a pair of jeans. She flicked through a pile of T-shirts, trying to work out if any of them were cool.

"What are you doing?" asked Ma Ma.

"Finding something decent to wear to the party."

"But . . . have you not noticed the dresses I have laid out?"

Ma Ma seemed genuinely confused. Peijing felt sorry for her. Ma Ma had made an effort to be kind to Peijing over the last few days. Ma Ma disappeared out of the bedroom. She came back with a photo album and flipped through the memories of their old life, until she found the one.

"See. Aren't you pretty?"

Peijing did not agree. While all the girls in the back row stood petitely in their party dresses and the ones at the front sat with their legs tucked ladylike underneath them, Peijing didn't seemed to have gotten the same notice. There she was in the photo right in the middle, cross-legged, with the skirt of the blue satin dress bunched inside her lap, exposing her bare legs and knees. She was also squinting at the sun.

Peijing was, though, immediately saddened to see all her former classmates. She had been friends with all of them and they had invited one another to birthday parties. Ma Ma had gone along too as the mums liked to get together and chat over a plate of *kueh* and chat. Ma Ma was not invited to this party. But Ma Ma also thought all the other mums in Peijing's class were strangers. Peijing herself had struggled to make any new friends beyond Joanna, and Gem was definitely just using her to get an alpaca petting farm— she had actually said so.

"That blue dress is the best thing you own," said Ma Ma.

"I'm going to wear something else," said Peijing.

Ma Ma was so shocked she sat down silently on the bed.

That was when Peijing picked up the blue dress and put it on. She tried to let out the sigh held so tightly inside of her slowly so it wouldn't make a noise. Biju came running into the room, and Ma Ma pinned her down so she could put the other dress on her, despite her protests.

Peijing tried putting her hair into one ponytail on the side of her head, but she had so much hair it was more like a horse tail than a ponytail. It pulled on the side of her head and hurt. She put it back down again. She grimaced and grew nervous.

"Have a good time," said Ma Ma, as the girls followed Ba Ba out the front door. Peijing pricked up her ears; these words were new for Ma Ma. She couldn't help notice how sad Ma Ma looked framed in the doorway as they left, almost as if she wanted to reach out and couldn't.

The two foil balloons tied onto the letter box bobbing in the wind indicated that this was the party house. Peijing's stomach felt like those two balloons. She still had not told Gem that she was bringing her little sister.

"Do you want me to come inside too?" asked Ba Ba. Peijing shook her head and quickly got out of the car. Joanna had given her a quick rundown of the rules of Australian big-kid parties, and this definitely included no parents. She had also learned that it was custom for something to occur to the fruit punch called "spiking" and that a bottle might be spun, and you had to kiss someone.

"In that case I better go," said Ba Ba. "Have a good time." If Peijing didn't know better, she would have thought it looked like disappointment on his face. As he drove away, she felt for a moment that she wanted to run after his car and demand to get back in. But instead she took a deep breath and entered the open gate with Biju.

Peijing was glad that the first person she saw was Joanna, huddled by herself, along the side of the house. She was dressed as she had described, in her oversize purple blouse and denim dungarees, her hair tied to one side with a purple scrunchie. Joanna was glad to see Peijing and Biju too.

"Remember the time we fell off my bike and completely missed the dog poop?" she asked, and Biju giggled.

Gem, on the other hand, was not so glad to see Biju.

"I said it was a big-kid party—why did you bring your little sister?" she said, marching up to their group. "And who dressed you? Your mum?"

Gem was very mature in a shirt with a giant tiger's head on it that revealed one spaghetti-strapped shoulder. She had done something to her hair to make it all frizzy like Maggi instant noodles.

"You will like Biju," said Joanna. "She's really funny. And I think both of them look really cute, like something from a storybook."

"Did you bring me a present, Joanna?" snapped Gem, changing the subject.

Joanna's smile disappeared, and she looked down at her feet.

"Here's your present," said Peijing, holding it out to Gem. "It's from all three of us."

Gem looked at the strange present Peijing held out, a small red envelope with gold foreign letters on it. Gem took it from Peijing with two fingers, as if it might attack her.

Usually, if Peijing were given an *ang bao* herself,

she would say, "Thank you," and then hide it away, looking inside it later, at a discreet moment. Gem opened it on the spot and shook out the contents. She smiled widely in surprise at the money.

"Well, what are you all waiting for? Come with me," said Gem in a voice that suddenly seemed kinder. "I have fruit punch and some potato chips on the table. Mummy is going to bring out the sausage rolls and party pies in a moment."

The three of them followed Gem and looked in awe as the brick path opened up to a big backyard. Standing huddled in the middle of a low metal railing were three alpacas. One white, one caramel, and one chocolate. A smile and a sigh formed on Peijing's lips.

"It's like the real Little World!" whispered Biju, and Peijing knew that her sister would be drawing nothing else but alpacas for weeks to come. Peijing reached out her hand and touched the long neck of one of them; it felt curly and strange. The animal took a step back in fright, and so did Peijing. Then it stepped forward and allowed her to touch its head. She turned to talk to Joanna, but Joanna had already moved to the food table.

The hot food had come out, and Joanna was standing in front of it, nervously swallowing.

"Do you think it'd be okay if I ate something?"

Joanna asked. She looked around as if she expected someone to say no or laugh at her. But all their other classmates were preoccupied with choosing what music tapes to put into the boom box.

"I'm sure," said Peijing, shrugging her shoulders. "We're going to eat too."

Joanna looked relieved and started piling food on her plate so fast that Peijing almost laughed and said jokingly, "Surely you can't eat that much!" But surely enough, it went at record speed down the slight girl's throat.

Peijing hadn't tried either of the two foods before, but she put two of each onto a plate for her and Biju and squeezed tomato sauce on the top like Joanna had done. She took a bite of the sausage roll. It was good. Peijing ate the whole thing and decided she could eat another. The meat pie, on the other hand . . . had a strange gooey brown center. Peijing wasn't so sure about it.

The music started blasting, and it was a song that Peijing recognized as being one of Miss Lena's aerobics songs, so it made her feel a lot more comfortable being at the party. At this point, the other girls came over to stand at the table, and Peijing noticed Joanna melt away toward the alpacas.

Joanna, who was dressed just like all the other

girls. Joanna, who should be like all the other girls . . . but was somehow not.

It should be Peijing, dressed like a doll when she was far too old, trying to hide away. But Peijing was happy to stand where she was—satin dress or no satin dress—because she missed hanging around a large group like she used to do.

The girls were staring intently at her, and her face reddened. She wondered if the punch was "spiked" and if anyone was going to play spin the bottle. Gem had only invited the girls in her class. And Jimmy. 'Cos Jimmy was not gross.

They were definitely judging her dress. Part of her wanted to back away and join Joanna. She felt herself retreat into a dark recess on the inside.

"Who dressed you?" asked one of her classmates. "Your mother?"

"Yes," said Peijing. She went quiet. She counted to five. Scrabbling blindly in the darkness inside of her, she found something.

"Yes," repeated Peijing. "My mother bought this dress for me from a very special department store called OG. It's actually very expensive, you know. It's made of real silk, just like they used to wear in the imperial court."

It wasn't true, of course—Peijing suspected it was

made of something synthetic as it was always itchy. She looked directly at the girl closest to her.

"The parties I used to go to—all the girls dressed like this. In fact, if I went to a party dressed like you, everyone would think I was wearing pajamas."

What Peijing had found inside her was her voice.

The girl who had spoken to Peijing looked quickly down at her shirt and jeans. She could see the other sets of eyes darting around at one another.

"What else happens at these parties you go to?" asked a girl from the back. Peijing recognized her as a quiet girl from class, a reader and a writer and a dreamer.

"Oh, lots of food. We have noodles and fried rice and chicken wings and curry puffs and coconut milk jellies. It's always a feast. And there's so much left over we take the rest home to have for dinner."

"Is it special fried rice, like at our local Chinese restaurant?" asked a different girl.

"Are there Hokkien noodles?" said another. "They're my favorite."

"Yup. I used to go to these parties all the time, sometimes once on a Saturday and then on a Sunday." Peijing picked up a sausage roll, squirted tomato sauce along it, and bit into it. The other girls picked up the sausage rolls and meat pies and bit into them too. They stared at one another. Some sort of mutual respect—if not yet friendship—was reached then, and everyone, not just Peijing, felt good about it.

There was a sudden yell, and all eyes turned toward the alpaca pen. Biju was lying on her back, flat on the ground. Peijing gasped and ran over.

"Biju, what is wrong?"

"She just slipped on a wet bit of grass," said Joanna. "I think she's okay."

The two of them grabbed hold of a hand each and peeled Biju off the grass. Biju came up . . . and so did the huge smudge of alpaca poo on the back of her dress.

"Oh, no!" exclaimed Joanna, and she started to laugh until tears rolled down her face.

"Poor Biju," said Peijing, and she held her nose. She also sighed. She had only just convinced her classmates she was worth talking to, but now they might change their minds. Trust Biju!

"That is disgusting!" said Gem as she came out of the house carrying a tray of mini quiches. She hurriedly put the food down at the table.

"Come on, let's get you changed, then." Gem held out her hand, and Biju took it.

Biju came out of the house later, wearing a pair of denim shorts and a shirt of Gem's that on Biju looked comically but fashionably oversize. Peijing chatted to some of the girls in her class, and they seemed genuinely interested in her.

An ice cream cake was brought out by Gem's mother, and everyone sang "Happy Birthday." There was white bread cut into triangles, slathered in margarine, and covered in sprinkles. Peijing was given a rectangular biscuit covered in chocolate, still cold from the fridge, and she put it whole into her mouth.

Joanna said it was called a Tim Tam, and suddenly, like a revelation, Peijing understood what that strange Little World code, 24 x 200g Arnott's Tim Tams, meant. It was a missing puzzle piece slotted in. It was also the most delicious thing she had ever tasted. Peijing forgot about the chocolate from home.

It wasn't long until Ba Ba came to pick them up, and Peijing realized she had actually had a really good time. In fact, a wonderful time.

Sitting with Biju in the back seat, Peijing felt that the day had put a coat of joy around her, that she was invincible against any bad things that might be happening at home. She looked in the party bag Gem had given each of them to take home and carefully inspected a mini lip gloss and an eraser that smelled like candy floss.

And it was infectious. Even Ba Ba seemed to have

forgotten about any of his worries in that moment, tapping his hands on the steering wheel to the tune of the music on the radio. Peijing tuned out the sound of Biju's voice talking on and on about alpacas. Deep inside, she let out a great sigh of relief. It was tiring to hold on to and feel so much all the time. It felt so good to breathe.

"Guess which animal didn't place at all in the race?" asked Biju.

"Tell me," said Ba Ba, sounding intrigued.

"The cat! The rat had promised to wake the cat up in time for the race, but it didn't—on purpose! That is why they are enemies to this day. Whoopsies."

Biju took the paper rat and fed it to the paper cat, laughing all the while.

"Whoopsies, into the stomach, yum yum."

"Don't forget I'm born in the year of the rat," cautioned Ba Ba, but he was smiling. He smiled a lot these days.

CHAPTER TWENTY-THREE

Ba Ba relaxed into his role of a hands-on dad in a way that surprised everyone. But at the same time, Peijing was beginning to understand the capabilities of human nature. Ba Ba had just never had an opportunity to do anything except work seven days a week, and now he was discovering that life held much more. He learned how to pack lunches so that Ma Ma could sleep in, and, on Fridays, he made bologna and cheese sandwiches. It was an awful sandwich, but nobody told him.

He walked Peijing and Biju to school and back under that pottery-blue sky. Peijing asked if they could walk themselves sometime. Ba Ba said maybe later, probably much later. There were still things he wasn't quite ready to let go of. Just yet.

After school he would sit with Ah Ma and watch Peijing and Biju work on the Little World until he seemed to understand it as well as they did. He learned about the passing of the seasons, the rhythm of the lands, the way each animal played a part in shaping the ecosystems. He realized why some animals always stayed in the same place, why some went back to where they themselves were born in order to raise their young, and why some left their homes to make new homes across the other side of the world, never to return. And he was amazed.

These days felt like the glory days of old, even though those days never existed. The box was filled up to the top now, and Peijing had to keep pressing it down to make it all fit. She was scared in her heart that sooner or later another Extinction would occur, and for that that she would be unable to forgive Ma Ma. Deep down inside, Peijing had the dreadful thought that if the Little World wasn't able to adapt to Australia and suddenly disappeared overnight, then what did that mean for her?

Biju drew nothing but paddocks and filled them up with alpacas.

"Ah Ma will get better soon," Peijing would tell Biju when she became visibly scared by the confusing things Ah Ma would say. Sweet young Biju, still trusting in the words of those older than her, believed her big sister.

Sometimes Ah Ma became lost. Sometimes Ah Ma would tell sad stories from her past in startlingly clear detail. Sometimes she said she was okay when she did not look okay at all, and, when Peijing tried to find out what was wrong, Ah Ma had forgotten who she was again.

There was no further mention of the special home.

Biju was for the most part happy. She was growing and thriving in her new environment, much better than Peijing was. Biju had forgotten almost everything about her old home and was even getting all the names of her cousins and relatives mixed up. Peijing for the most part still remembered everyone, and in her dreams all the faces of those she had left behind loomed individual and clear.

"Don't anyone forget about today!" hollered Biju at breakfast. "Today I am the sun! I need my yellow outfit! Ma Ma, are you coming to watch me? Ba Ba, are you coming too? What about you, Ah Ma?" Biju's foot tapped nervously against the leg of the dining table.

Ma Ma did not say anything. Ba Ba was busy trying to look at the nutritional information that was printed very small on a box of brightly colored cereal. Ah Ma was concentrating hard on eating the cereal, which had been soaked in milk so it had turned to mush and was therefore safe for Ah Ma to eat. Peijing wanted to stand up and quickly usher Biju through all the motions of the morning so that they could just get going.

There were still things in the past that Peijing remembered in great detail. The feel of the Mother Bear mask on her face. The way she felt when she looked in the audience and did not see her parents there. The way her heart sank. The hidden tears that streamed down, thankfully hidden behind that paper plate mask.

She knew that stories from the past had a habit of repeating themselves.

"Ma Ma, you should come and watch Biju today," Peijing said, and it came out really loud.

"Jing-Jing, don't speak to your mother in that voice," said Ba Ba.

Peijing stared at her father. He hadn't called her by that pet name since she was little and the idea of having a child was still novel to him.

Ma Ma stood up and left the table without a sound.

"Great one!" complained Biju. "It's your fault if Ma Ma doesn't come and watch me!"

"As the old Chinese proverb goes," says Ah Ma, "'Love shows itself as naturally as the sunflower faces the sun.'"

Peijing couldn't stand it any longer, so she left the table herself, still taking great pains to excuse herself politely. She was about to barge into the bedroom when she noticed Ma Ma sitting on Biju's bed.

She stopped and peeked inside. On Ma Ma's lap was a creased yellow party dress that Peijing had not seen in a long time. It used to belong to her, before it was passed down to Biju, who in turn had a tantrum about hand-me-downs and refused to wear it. She was surprised Ma Ma had kept it.

"I was a person too, before I became Ma Ma," she said, not looking up. Peijing was shocked her mother could tell she was there. Joanna had casually mentioned that all mothers had eyes in the back of their heads, and Peijing had thought it was just a strange saying used in Australia, but maybe it was true.

She approached cautiously and sat down.

"Before I met your father, I worked in a printing factory. Our most profitable items were counterfeit playing cards, but as it was illegal, we had to quickly make sure we hid all the evidence when the authorities came to check the factory." Ma Ma smiled. "We just said we printed books."

Peijing had heard many stories, but she had never heard this story before.

"The best thing was that all the workers got free

books! I read and kept each one! I left them all behind in an old suitcase when I moved out of my childhood home to marry your father. I don't know what ever happened to them." Ma Ma's eyes became misty.

It came as a shock to realize that Ma Ma was once a great reader. Peijing had come to accept that her mother couldn't read, but it was just that Ma Ma couldn't read English. She could read Chinese fine.

"I think it might be time for me to get a job again. To find that person that used to be happy," said Ma Ma. She smoothed down the yellow dress and placed it down on the bed.

"I've discovered that there is an Asian Mart one bus stop away that is looking for casual staff. I don't mind stacking shelves or even learning to serve customers. What do you think?"

Peijing nodded slowly. It was strange to think of Ma Ma being someone other than the person who cooked and cleaned and sewed back Biju's loose buttons and did a thousand invisible things a day to keep the household together.

"Especially now that your father is helping around the house—although his cooking is a little strange!"

Peijing and Ma Ma laughed at the same time, and it felt good. It felt like they hadn't done anything together for a long time. Peijing was proud of her mother in that moment. Ma Ma was also a great warrior like Hua Mulan, going into her own personal battle. If Ba Ba and Ma Ma could cope for the better, then there was hope for her.

"I'm sorry I raised my voice at you at the table," Peijing told Ma Ma.

The Guos were a very honorable family with old traditions, and although they showed forgiveness in different ways, nobody had ever, until now, said the word "sorry."

"That's okay," said Ma Ma in surprise and put her hand on Peijing's shoulder.

Maybe, Peijing thought to herself, *I can start some new traditions too.*

"But I am sorry I won't be able to go and see Biju's play. I can't, not today," said Ma Ma. "I will next time, I promise."

Peijing was sad, but she was glad that, instead of remaining unspoken, Ma Ma was letting her feelings out, and that Ma Ma looked better for it.

Biju bounced on her heels, as nervous as a Hollywood actress embarking on her first major role. Ma Ma had ironed the yellow party dress and laid it out on the bed; Biju was staring at it as if she were still making up her mind on what she thought of it. Peijing braced for a tantrum, but Biju picked it up and slipped it over her head.

"You hate that dress," said Peijing.

Biju smoothed it down with her hands. "I changed my mind. Isn't that part of growing up?"

"Yes," admitted Peijing.

"Well, I like it because it belonged to you," said Biju.

Peijing smiled and felt a profound sense of love.

"It'll bring me luck," said Biju.

"You don't need luck because you'll be great."

For a second Peijing thought about ruffling up Biju's hair, like she'd seen some of her schoolmates' parents do as a sign of affection. But Biju had specifically brushed her hair a hundred times that morning, and now she had put on her golden crown, with its rays of uncooked spaghetti.

"How do I look?" Biju asked uncertainly, suddenly a child.

"Just like the sun," said Peijing.

School was much better since Gem's party. The girls in her class would smile and nod their heads in her direction now. Peijing knew that if she joined in their conversations and took more than a passing interest in what currently interested them all—the latest music, the latest fashion craze, the latest TV poster boy they had on their bedroom walls—she might be accepted into one of their groups. But Peijing found that none of them liked Joanna any better no matter how hard Joanna tried, so she drew away from them and stuck more closely to Joanna than ever.

Joanna would look in her direction and afterward say, "You should be friends with them; why are you friends with me?"

As if friendship were a journey in which you swapped current friends with better friends.

"Because you wanted to be friends with me first," replied Peijing.

Joanna smiled and asked to hold her hand, and Peijing knew for certain now, regardless of tradition, that touching was a good thing.

She found her friend sitting at the desk by herself that morning, her long blond hair forming curtains to block the world out.

"What happened to your face?" Peijing exclaimed in horror as she placed a package containing a breakfast bao on Joanna's desk. She took a step back without opening the paper napkin.

"I tripped and fell over," said Joanna hastily. "I'm a bit of a klutz."

"What is a klutz?" asked Peijing, unable to stop staring at the bruise on Joanna's cheek.

"It just means I'm clumsy, okay? I'm clumsy and I got hurt and I deserve it!" yelled Joanna, and the other students turned to look. Nobody laughed or whispered this time.

"I'm sorry," said Peijing. "It looks painful."

"Maybe if my dad had a job, then he wouldn't be like this," said Joanna tearfully. "He says he would have a job if people didn't come to this country and take them all away."

Peijing was so confused. Ba Ba got his job because they opened a new office in Australia, and they made the new job just for him. He didn't walk into a bank like a robber and steal an innocent person's hard-earned job.

"Time to form a line and go to the lunch area," said Miss Lena. "The kindergartners are giving a special performance at assembly this morning."

"I'm sorry too. It's not your fault," said Joanna, and she grabbed on to Peijing's sleeve as they both stood up.

"You should tell Miss Lena about it," said Peijing.

"I'm sure she doesn't want to hear about a silly accident." Joanna tried to laugh it off, but Peijing did not laugh with her.

It looked like Joanna was going to say something more, but then they got caught in the crowd and separated. Peijing found herself carried to the front. She looked all around. She wanted to say something, but Joanna had been jostled to the back of the line.

Peijing knew it wasn't a silly accident. The whole story spread out as clear as if she was seeing it whole from the moon. She left her place at the front, ran all the way to the back, and caught Joanna's hand just in time.

"It's not silly," said Peijing breathlessly.

"I'm not my father," said Joanna with fear in her voice. "I don't want to be."

"You don't have to be," said Peijing. "You are not your father or your mother or anyone else. You are yourself. If you let yourself be. It was you who taught me that."

Joanna nodded tearfully.

Miss Lena stepped out of the classroom, closing the door behind her. She looked at the side of Joanna's face, and her eyes, rimmed in electric blue, widened. Peijing held on tightly to Joanna's hand. Miss Lena ran her fingers through Joanna's long hair, and, when the girl turned to face her, Miss Lena smiled sadly.

"Once upon a time there was a monkey that hatched out of an egg made from stone. He broke into the Peach Garden of Immortality, went wild, and ate all the peaches in it. He was in deep trouble 'cos these peaches take a hundred years to ripen," said Biju, unfolding the paper orchard.

"But Buddha said the monkey could be forgiven if he could walk the length of Buddha's palm. Guess what happened?"

"What happened?" asked Peijing.

"Monkey didn't realize that Buddha's palm stretched on forever 'cos Buddha did so himself. So Buddha put him under a mountain for five hundred years to learn about patience. Cheeky monkey."

"Did he learn about patience?" asked Peijing.

"No," said Biju. "I think he just had lots of time to figure out that he was who he was."

Biju folded the orchard back up and stroked it lovingly.

CHAPTER TWENTY-FOUR

The whole school was already assembled on the concrete of the lunch area, as Miss Lena sat her class at the back with the rest of the older kids. A lot of excited parents with cameras were chatting to one another on the plastic chairs, and Peijing turned to glance at them briefly before she turned back with a heavy heart.

Maybe Biju would be too focused on her role to notice neither Ma Ma or Ba Ba were there. Peijing ran through all the excuses in her mind that she would tell her sister after the show. Then she stopped. She knew she would spend her entire life trying to protect her sister, but from behind the thick red curtains the kindergartners had set up, she caught a glimpse of a yellow skirt. She had to give her sister enough room to grow.

Mr. Brodie walked up onstage, and a hush descended over the audience. He thanked everyone for making the time to come, gestured toward the stage, and stepped to the side. The red velvet curtain drew open and everyone cheered and clapped.

A princess, a knight, and a king were revealed in the center of the stage.

A hand clasped onto Peijing's shoulder. She looked up to see Ba Ba standing there. Her face broke out into a surprised smile. Her eyes followed him as he went to sit with the other parents.

"That's my princess!" said the loud man next to Ba Ba.

Everyone said, "Shh."

Peijing turned eagerly back toward the stage.

"A new day begins," read the narrator from the oversize prop book.

In the very far left corner, crouched on the ground, was a girl dressed all in yellow, a gold crown of raw spaghetti on her head. She appeared to freeze, her eyes glued on the crowd. There was an awkward shuffling from the audience, a few coughs. Peijing was fearful that Biju's brief career as a famous actress had ended before it had even started.

But the girl in the yellow dress was just biding her time. From her position on the ground, she rose, yawned theatrically with a hand over her mouth, and stretched luxuriantly.

Then she almost slipped over in her stockinged feet.

Biju's eyes searched the audience frantically. Her eyes found and locked onto Peijing's. Her big sister gave her a nod and a smile. Biju nodded and smiled back. Standing straight with her arms firmly by her side, Biju took a sidestep. It was just as planned. The sun had successfully begun her journey.

Characters from the medieval court played out the story center stage. The princess was magnificent. The king did not cry. A kid playing a giant jousting stick provided comedic value. There were students playing big and small roles, human and animal roles, and everything in between. Characters moved on and off the stage. The only character that was on the stage at all times was the sun.

Peijing watched as Biju played her role with every single conviction in her body. From the way she smiled to the way she grew tired when she reached the middle of the stage and it became noon. The way she grew more tired as she was reaching her final destination on the right side of the stage.

"All the children are really good!" whispered one of the grown-ups sitting behind Peijing. "But I just can't take my eyes off that little sun!"

"Yes, the little sun! She does quite steal the show, doesn't she?"

Peijing's heart swelled with pride.

As the narrator announced the closing of the day, all eyes were on Biju. The sun stretched her arms out, yawned with great character, and then slowly set upon the play, curling up into a ball.

Peijing was the first to jump up off the concrete floor and start clapping. Students started standing up with her, and soon everyone was on their feet clapping and cheering.

All the students stood in a row across the stage and bowed together. Then they took a step forward individually and bowed. The king. The princess. Both halves of a horse. Biju's turn was last; she stepped forward and almost tripped again. She straightened in shock when she realized she was receiving the loudest cheer of them all. She grinned and bowed again, until Mr. Brodie gently told her she could now leave the stage.

Peijing looked all around. There was a vibration that moved the space around her. A hum that she could almost make out the words to. It sounded like the world was telling her that her sister was coming into her own person. She wondered if it was true that Biju would end up a Hollywood actress who would forget about her family and her humble beginnings one day.

Peijing turned to see Ba Ba behind her, giving a

standing ovation along with the other parents. He smiled at her with a twinkle in his eye, or was that a tear?

"Hey, come here," said Ba Ba to Biju, who broke free from her class and ran up to him all tense and jittery, like a shaken-up bottle of fizzy drink.

"I knew you would come," said Biju and did not understand how it could be any other way.

"I feel so lucky to be here instead of at work," said Ba Ba as Biju hugged him silently, her eyes closed.

"Even though it means all those people will have to wait longer for their community to be built?" asked Biju.

Ba Ba did not reply. He exchanged a look with Peijing, they connected, and she knew that they were thinking about how quickly circumstances could change. That he would have missed all of this if not for Ah Ma getting ill. But that none of them wanted Ah Ma to be ill at all.

"Peijing, I'm sorry I never went to any of your school performances," said Ba Ba as all the teachers tried to get everyone back into rows of two. The atmosphere had taken on a casual, social sheen. The different years broke down their formalities and mingled with one another, and nobody was in a hurry to get back to class.

"I just didn't know how important it was."

"It's okay," replied Peijing. Peijing was still sad that Ba Ba was not around to watch her perform in her own play when she was young, and maybe that pain would always be there. But she was touched that he was here now. It felt as though there was a possibility of a new beginning and of a new ending.

The feeling continued, permeating the corners of the classroom. Peijing thought she could see pieces of universe, dense and full of stars, sitting on top of the Encyclopaedia Britannica, on top of the aquarium, inside the jars of red water from the cochineal experiments. No one could really concentrate, so Miss Lena gave up and told everyone to work independently, as long as they could work quietly.

Peijing felt warm on the outside but strangely empty on the inside, as if something had detached itself from her and was now floating around in a vacuum.

She sat with Joanna at lunch, and they felt lonely together. Joanna seemed so tired and disheartened, as though the world had taken away what was good about life. She let Peijing hold her hand in silence as they watched the magical motes dance in the light.

Every single day, in her head, Peijing imagined the two of them stepping out of the magic tree and the world suddenly changing. Sometimes it was a completely different fantasy world, where feathered cats prowled the jungles and flying whales thundered and cut through the sky like water, one where the two of them could stay forever in a dream. Sometimes it was the real world, but one that felt like hope and filled them with a sense of confidence. But always, when they stepped out, it was the same old world.

Peijing looked at the bruise on Joanna's left cheek.

She looked at Joanna's right shoe, still held by the elastic band that Ma Ma put there.

"I would still like to invite you over to my place, but my dad would get angry," said Joanna.

"I would still like to invite you over too, but my mum wouldn't like it," said Peijing.

"When I have kids one day," said Joanna, "I will let them have their friends over all the time, and I won't punish them just for existing."

"You didn't fall down on your face, did you?" asked Peijing.

"No," said Joanna.

Peijing did not say *I knew it* or *I told you so*. She just sat and listened to her friend talk.

• • •

"The bad news," said Miss Lena, "is that the two of you are the only students not going on the camping trip."

Peijing and Joanna looked down at their feet. They would both still have to go to school while everyone else was having fun on the trip. Peijing didn't mind going to school—she had grown to like it—but she had wanted to know what it was like to sleep under the stars in the Western Australian Wild-flower Country.

"The good news is that I'm not going either," said Miss Lena with a grin. "So you are both stuck with me."

Peijing looked over at Joanna.

"I'm actually volunteering to stay behind because sleeping under the stars is not all it's cut out to be. Not to mention what all the wildflowers will do to my sinuses. Then there's awful camping food and shared toilets. I'd rather much stay at home in my comfy bed—with my own toilet!"

Miss Lena was saying the same thing as Ma Ma, really, when Ma Ma had told Peijing she wasn't allowed to go. But at the same time it was different. Peijing and Joanna couldn't help giggling. They thought of Miss Lena and her snake-print court shoes trampling through the mud.

That was when Peijing learned the might of words. She had control over how to say things. And she promised herself that she would use them like a superpower, changing negative phrases into positive ones, flipping sentences around so that they turned frowns into smiles. Banishing the bad beliefs. Defeating the thoughts that damaged.

Miss Lena giggled as well. Then her eyes settled on the bruise on Joanna's face, and she went quiet. She tried to keep her hand away, but in the end she couldn't, and Miss Lena stood there with Joanna's face in her fingers. Their teacher looked like she was about to cry, but Joanna had a serene smile on her face, glad to be noticed.

NEW MOON

"Rawr," said Biju, "do you like my nian?"

"It's very . . . colorful," said Peijing, not wanting to pass further judgment on her sister's artistic integrity.

"Well, it was said to have the head of a lion and the body of a dog and to have been as large as an elephant," replied Biju solemnly.

"Did it wail like a baby?"

"No," said Biju. Sometimes her sister could be so presumptuous.

"But during winter, when food was scarce, the nian would come into the villages and eat children. So everyone would go and hide. The ancient times were horrible times."

"Lucky we don't have people in the Little World," said Peijing.

"Oh, it also ate whatever animal it came across," replied Biju.

Peijing frowned and pushed the cardboard box a little farther away from the nian.

"But one day, this clever villager had a bright idea."

CHAPTER TWENTY-FIVE

Ba Ba cooked spaghetti with tomato sauce and pieces of Spam. He called it Spamghetti. Peijing, Biju, and Ah Ma loved Spamghetti. Ma Ma said it was interesting.

"Aren't I a star?" asked Biju and repeated it over and over again just to hear the answer.

"I am sorry to have missed your show," said Ah Ma. She had tomato sauce on her chin but did not notice.

"Don't worry, there will be more!" exclaimed Biju. "Mr. Brodie said that I am a natural and I should join an after-school drama class. Ba Ba, can I join a drama class?"

"Why not?" said Ba Ba, catching the spirit. "I'll have to try to juggle my hours after I go back to work, but we can give it a go."

"Yes!" said Biju, scrunching both hands into fists.

Peijing looked down at the table and thought about how she'd failed that music test because she was sure that nobody would take her or even want her to go to an extracurricular music class. Her fingers traced the wood, around and around.

Maybe the firstborn was supposed to make sacrifices for the secondborn. She tried to look out the window for the jade rabbit so she could ask him about his own sacrifice and whether it was just as painful. But the moon was in the middle of being reborn and was only a tiny sliver of silver hanging in the sky.

She went to her bedroom to stare at the flyer for the poster competition and ached for something of her own.

As was the routine now, Peijing helped Ba Ba wash the dishes, and he would give her a dollar, even though he said she was not allowed to buy a bike. She was allowed to spend it on art supplies. Peijing knew that Ba Ba would buy what she asked for, but somehow it was different to buy it for herself.

She never went back to the school supplies store next to the school, but she found a news agency that was more than happy to sell her card stock, smudgy graphite pencils, and glitter pens with galaxies swirling inside.

· · ·

With the chores done, Peijing and Biju closed the bedroom and dragged the Little World out from under the bed. It was overfilled like a treasure chest. There were so many animals on the land and so many goats on the mountains and so many fish in the sea that it made both their eyes water.

Extinctions appeared to be, well, extinct.

But there was something missing.

Biju started drawing another alpaca to add to her flock, but she seemed uninterested. She talked mostly about what her teacher Mr. Brodie called the "performing arts," which, unlike "visual arts," was not just using your hands to create something but using your entire body. Biju thought it suited her better.

Peijing picked the rabbit up, still crinkled but back on the moon. She wondered why he was still the only rabbit in the world when every other animal came in at least a pair. She thought about drawing him a friend, but her mind wandered, and she found herself unable to enter their shared world, her eyes and ears on the bedroom door instead.

What was missing was the rest of the family.

Biju and Peijing both realized they'd rather be out there than hidden in here.

So the Little World, hardly unpacked, was

pushed back under the bed and the bedroom door thrown open.

The night relaxed and unfolded like a hand.

Biju weaved through the house, using her body to express herself, telling an imaginary story only she knew. Peijing stuck closer to the walls and peeked through the open door of her parents' rooms, attracted to the lamplight.

Ma Ma was at her wardrobe, taking out one coat hanger and examining the two-piece outfit on it before putting it back and taking out another.

"You should wear them again," said Peijing, coming in uninvited and touching the white pleated skirt with the colored spots. The one that Ma Ma had worn on the airplane to come to Australia. It seemed so long ago.

Maybe one day she will have been in Australia for so long it would feel like she'd never lived anywhere else. Peijing was still unsure whether this was a good or bad thing.

"I am," said Ma Ma. "I'm going for a job interview at the Asian Mart next week. They want someone to start straightaway. I'm just not sure if I'm that person."

Ma Ma looked nervous.

"I am sure you can be that person," said Peijing

and then quickly pursed her lips together. She wasn't supposed to talk to adults as though she was an adult herself; that was dishonorable. Well, it was dishonorable back home, anyway.

But Ma Ma didn't chastise her over it. Instead, she just said, "I hope so," made her concentrating face, and kept flipping through her wardrobe.

Peijing was glad that Ma Ma was slowly adapting. She was glad that Ma Ma was beginning to think of her as an adult. But then Peijing thought about the mooncake again, the celebration with family, that golden egg yolk, and she didn't want to gain something new at the expense of losing that.

The open night was suddenly punctuated with the sound of the front door banging.

Peijing and Ma Ma looked at each other and rushed out the room.

There at the front door stood Ah Ma. She had managed to unlatch and open the front door, but it had slammed shut. Now Ah Ma was trying to unlock it again.

"What are you doing, Ah Ma?!" Peijing exclaimed.

"Why, I'm just trying to go home," replied Ah Ma. "What are you doing in this strange house all by yourself? Where is your mother?"

"She's right here next to me," replied Peijing.

"I see," said Ah Ma.

"What is happening here?" said Ba Ba as he came down the hallway with Biju in tow.

Ah Ma's hand reached out to open the front door. Ba Ba put his hand over hers. Ah Ma yelled in fright.

"What is wrong? Is this why Ah Ma needs to go to a special home?" The words burst from Biju's mouth before she bursts into tears a second later.

"The mid-autumn moon is the brightest; with every festival the homesickness multiples!" exclaimed Ah Ma.

"Let's get you to bed," said Ma Ma firmly and managed to get Ah Ma to follow her. She put her arm over Ah Ma's frail shoulders and led her away.

Peijing sat with Biju back in the bedroom, and nothing she said proved to be soothing to her sister because she knew just as little. And Biju could tell. This was not the same girl who could be fooled with excuses as easily as she was once fooled by Extinctions.

Peijing was secretly relieved when Ma Ma came into the room to sit with Biju. Sometimes only a mother will do. Although it was a sacrifice to her, because she needed her mother too, Peijing walked out of the room and left the two of them together.

. . .

Peijing sat in the corner of the bathroom on the plastic bathing chair and watched Ba Ba standing in front of the mirror. She hadn't done that since she was the same age as Biju and didn't know how to respect people's privacy.

Ba Ba was finally going to do it this time, even though he had been talking about it for the longest time. He pulled out the electric clippers and plugged them in. They made an ominous buzz.

"I want to know about the special home," said Peijing.

Ba Ba was going to shave all his hair off. He had been turning gray for years, but now it had come to the point where he was completely gray. The clippers buzzed off a section of his hair.

"Ah Ma is not going to get better, is she?" said Peijing. It echoed off the pink tiles. They did not look edible today.

"No," said Ba Ba. "I'm going to be honest with you because I think you are old enough now. We will have to make some hard decisions. One of them might be to put Ah Ma in a place where she can be cared for properly. It doesn't mean Ah Ma can't have a good life, do you understand?"

"But what about family honor?" Peijing blurted. The words pushed up hard against her throat. Burned the back of her mouth.

She was taught to believe that when your parents become old it is their children's duty to look after them. That when Peijing was born, Ma Ma, Ba Ba, and Ah Ma all looked at her with the whole of the moon in their hearts, and that she needed to reflect that moon back in their waning years.

Ba Ba ran the clipper down the center of his head, leaving a shaved strip. Peijing didn't know whether to laugh or cry.

"I tried my best," said Ba Ba. "I made the decision for all of us to come here so that I could work five days a week instead of seven. So that I could come home at a good hour at five o'clock. I wanted us to be a family, Ah Ma included."

Peijing thought about the sacrifice Ba Ba had to make himself. She knew that Ba Ba could have one day become the most important person in his company back in Singapore if he had stayed.

"But sometimes we have to say to ourselves that we cannot fulfill that honor."

Peijing nodded even though she did not feel that way.

"Ah Ma will go to a place where carers can make sure she doesn't escape and get hurt."

Ba Ba's head was completely bald now, all the hair on the ground.

"What do you think? Do I look like a coconut?" he asked, turning around.

Peijing smiled through the tears in her eyes.

"The clever villager figured out that the nian had its weaknesses. It was scared of loud noises and the color red, so he suggested they try to defeat the monster together," said Biju.

"But nobody wanted to do it. They were all too scared and just wanted to hide inside their houses instead."

"Well, I think that's silly," puffed Peijing. "That's not going to solve the problem, is it?"

"Oh, I think people would rather let their children be eaten," said Biju and grinned with all of her teeth.

"So, what changed?"

"The nian started eating adults, too."

CHAPTER TWENTY-SIX

Miss Lena and her two remaining students waved goodbye to the bus taking everyone camping, and then headed back into the school to carry on as normal. Miss Lena still taught the class like she always did. At aerobics time, they still trooped down to the lunch area. Their teacher became a superhero in blue-and-pink Lycra who moved to the soundtrack of the latest hit songs, and Peijing and Joanna moved with her as a trio.

But there was a change in the air. A certain relaxed summer vibe crept in. Peijing thought again about how strange it was that it was mid-autumn when they'd left Singapore, but here, instead of heading toward winter, it was the other way around. Australia was indeed upside down like everyone said it was.

On Tuesday, Miss Lena brought in an electric frying pan and a videocassette. She showed them how to cook dried corn kernels in vegetable oil, and both girls stared in surprise at how the little hard seeds split open and turned inside out to show the world what they really had on the inside. They sweetened the popcorn with icing sugar and added a drop of pink food coloring. Joanna ate so much that her belly ached.

They sat down on beanbags and watched a movie about a war in space where the baddies blew up planets with giant laser beams and the goodies defeated them using a special power deep inside of them, and it made Peijing cry ugly tears because she was overwhelmed by the concept that people were always fighting over something. That, even in a future world full of technology, good people still faced death.

But the goodies beat the baddies in the end, and everyone got medals. Joanna said it was the best movie she had ever seen.

Miss Lena wheeled the TV and VCR back to the technology room, and Peijing quietly sat by herself and sketched space princesses. When Miss Lena came back, she sat down next to Joanna and they talked quietly together. It was mostly Joanna who talked; Miss Lena just wiped tears off her own face with a tissue.

"You are brave," Peijing said to Joanna.

"I'm not," said Joanna.

"Sometimes the bravest thing anyone can do is to talk about their problems," said Peijing. "And not just keep it on the inside."

"I felt good after telling Miss Lena," said Joanna. "Suddenly, I'm not afraid anymore."

"You still deserve to be put on the moon, for everyone to see. Like the jade rabbit," said Peijing. even though she wasn't sure yet of what he had done. Just that he got to live happily ever after. She hoped that they would too.

On Thursday, Miss Lena used the time to install a huge map of the world that covered almost one whole wall in the classroom. Peijing and Joanna sat beneath it, studying all the countries and cities that existed, and they were surprised to find so many places they had never heard of before. They tried to find their homes, but their town was just one tiny dot on the map.

"We can escape," said Peijing. "Let's pick three places each, and one day we will go there."

Joanna pointed to the Arctic waters around Greenland, Canada, and Russia, where the narwhals lived. Peijing pointed to the Fujian and Jiangxi provinces in China, and to Taiwan, places where Ah Ma said her ancestors had lived. They made up stories and discussed what they would have in their suitcases. Maybe it would be best to travel light with nothing but a passport full of stamps, two changes of clothing, and a warm sweater.

Joanna revealed that visitors had come to her house last night and she seemed excited about it because the house hadn't had visitors for a long time, even though they wore government badges and didn't bring any gifts of food or drink. Her father was not happy about it.

It seemed simple to escape the confines of where one lived when it was just a tiny dot, not so easy when real life loomed enormous and unavoidable.

At the end of the week, after four days and nights, the students all came back late Friday afternoon. Miss Lena said they should all work on an assignment about wildflowers, but the whole class moaned, and Miss Lena said, "Fine, how about you all write a story about your adventures instead?" Miss Lena told Peijing and Joanna they were allowed to do silent reading. Peijing wondered if she had the courage to ask her about the Look Before You Dive art competition, if they had decided the winners yet, since it was quiet and nobody was talking. But sometimes it felt like silence was harder to break through than noise.

. . .

Then it was finally the weekend. Ba Ba surprised everyone by taking them on their first outing ever to an enormous park on top of the highest peak of the city. They looked down at the little skyscrapers and buildings below. Pejing and Biju tried to see their home through the coin-operated binocular viewer, but the city was so spread out and so flat they weren't sure if they were looking in the right direction. The cars on the freeway looked like toys.

Ah Ma didn't try to wander off but was instead happy to admire the Australian wildflowers. She started telling stories about all the gardens she had visited in the past with an amazing amount of clarity. Peijing's heart once again told her that Ah Ma was going to be fine, but she knew it didn't sit right with her head.

Attracted by a pink-and-white van with a picture of an ice cream on the side, Peijing and Biju were surprised that, unlike the vendors along Orchard Road at home, the ice cream didn't come sandwiched between two pieces of sweet bread; instead it was a soft serve in a cone. But it was a delicious surprise.

"I got the job at the Asian Mart working the weekends," Ma Ma told Peijing as they licked the soft serve that melted onto the sides of their hands.

"Which outfit are you going to wear? The white skirt with the colored spots?" asked Peijing.

"It's at an Asian Mart," said Ma Ma, and she shrugged. "I think it would be more practical to wear a blouse and jeans."

Peijing was once again surprised, but she agreed it was for the best.

She asked Ba Ba if she and Biju could walk to and from school by themselves now. Ba Ba finally said yes, but only from school as a trial. He said that he would be back at work soon and if Ma Ma ended up working during the weekdays that the girls could also learn how to let themselves into the house.

Ma Ma looked worried.

Ba Ba left out where Ah Ma fit into any of this.

Peijing believed she was the only one who noticed.

Monday came and everything was the same again, but everything had changed.

Peijing felt like she was finally settled into school. Although she still thought about her old school from time to time, she no longer felt that ache and sickness that came with missing something badly.

Joanna came with news, and she told Peijing first.

"I'm leaving," she said. "I'm going to a new school."

Peijing stared at Joanna and the bruise on her face that had faded to an unnatural pale violet and jade green. The rubber band around her shoe had snapped, leaving the sole to flap around sadly again.

"I am going to go live with my grandmother who lives up in the hills. The visitors with the government badges said so."

"How am I going to see you again?" said Peijing, a lump forming in her throat.

"You can come visit me. My granny has a big house on stilts that sits right on the side of the hill. It has a wraparound veranda and the gardens are filled with flowers and birds. It's not that far, only a short car trip away. Although when you go up the hill your ears will pop."

Peijing listened, but it was as though she wasn't really hearing Joanna.

"Please? Granny is an artist. She will let us use her special oil paints. We can look out the big bay window in her studio and see the old eucalyptus trees. And we can bake cookies. Granny has the best recipes. . . ."

Peijing shook her head. She wouldn't be allowed.

Joanna stopped talking, and the fantasy hanging between them evaporated.

"When are you leaving?" Peijing asked.

"Today is my last day," replied Joanna. "Granny will pick me up this evening. Then I will go to the new school in the hills."

It felt like Joanna was moving to the mountains on the other side of the world.

Peijing did not believe her little world could stretch so far to encompass where Joanna was going, even though it was only a short car ride away.

"I want us still to be friends," said Joanna.

Peijing had that dread in her stomach that if she let Joanna go now that she would never get Joanna back. That when she was much older, and she tried to search for Joanna Polonaise, she would never find the real Joanna. Just a poodle groomer from Tasmania who happened to have the same name.

There was a difference to Joanna that was immediately noticeable. It was if a great weight had been lifted off her shoulders and Joanna half soared, half danced through the day as if in a dream. While Joanna threatened to float away like a balloon, Peijing felt heavy on the ground, like a stone. But there was no way Peijing could, or wanted to, hold her down.

Miss Lena would glance at Joanna throughout the day and smile to herself. Knowing that Joanna was leaving, the entire class—hostile or unbothered by her previously—decided that they were going to miss her after all. Everyone stood in two rows facing each other and formed an archway with their arms for Joanne to run through. There were cheers, and some of the girls in the class hugged her for the first time. Joanna looked like she had won a pageant. Miss Lena dismissed the class even though the bell hadn't rung yet.

"What are you working on?" Peijing asked shyly, approaching Miss Lena. She surprised herself; she never would have been this forward once. But she was changed in so many ways.

"I'm writing a letter to the school board," replied Miss Lena, biting her pen. "I want them to provide a breakfast for the kids that would otherwise go without. They will probably tell me they don't have the money, but I can try."

Miss Lena smiled at Peijing, and Peijing believed for a moment that her teacher's eye was the moon and reflected in it was a rabbit.

"We have to look out for each other," said Miss Lena. "If you ever find yourself in the position to do so. That is the greatest lesson I can teach you."

As they walked toward the bike stand, Peijing felt Joanna fade away like the bruise on her face. Joanna wheeled out her huge, rusty piece of junk that she locked up, "just in case anyone steals it as a joke," even though the bike wasn't a joke to her.

They both stood at the school gates.

It was now or never.

"Joanna, I don't want to lose you forever," said Peijing.

"It won't be forever!" Joanna laughed. "It's only a short car ride and then up a hill. Your ears might pop, like I said."

She stopped smiling because Peijing wasn't.

"Joanna, I want you to come over. Right now," said Peijing.

"Um, okay," replied Joanna. "I'll see if the reception will let me ring Granny, and I'll let her know."

"So that means you are coming over?"

"Of course!" said Joanna, and she grinned.

"We have to walk with Biju, though," groaned Peijing.

"That's fine by me," said Joanna.

The bell rang, signaling the end of the day. In the distance the sight and sounds of the other students exploded outward, a big bang, and the two of them weren't alone in their own space anymore.

"That's when the villagers changed their minds about the nian," explained Biju. "Adults sometimes don't mind if children get eaten, but they don't want to get eaten themselves."

"Fair enough," said Peijing, even though it didn't seem fair.

"So, with the guidance of the clever villager, they devised a plan. When the nian next came down from the mountains, they dressed brightly in red and, armed with firecrackers and drums, they made as much noise as they could."

CHAPTER TWENTY-SEVEN

Marching out the door of the creaky demountable classroom, Biju was enthusiastic to see both Peijing and Joanna waiting for her. She grinned at them. There was something different about Biju.

"You've got a new hole in your smile," said Joanna. "Maybe the tooth fairy will visit you tonight."

"What is the tooth fairy?" asked Biju. She walked up to Joanna and smiled widely again.

"Well, if you leave your old tooth under your pillow tonight, you might wake up to find it replaced with a coin."

"Where does this tooth fairy live?"

"In Granny's garden, I believe," replied Joanna earnestly.

"Are there different prices for different teeth?"

"I think the tooth fairy considers all teeth the same."

"What does the fairy do with the teeth?"

"Well . . . that I'm not entirely sure."

Biju grinned at the answer. She said she couldn't leave anything out for the tooth fairy as she had swallowed the tooth, and then she laughed maniacally.

These were the safe, innocent days that Peijing longed for, kicking along on the pavement and cutting through the park, having funny conversations. But it seemed like it was over already before it had begun. Peijing became more and more worried as they reached home. Biju stuck herself firmly to Joanna's side; she did not go running ahead today.

Then the moment Peijing dreaded arrived. They were home.

"I do like your house very much," said Joanna, hesitating and looking up at 4 Blueberry Street. "It's so big and nice." She smoothed down her school skirt.

"Come on," said Peijing and took her by the arm.

"Should I lock my bike up? No, I don't think so here. You live in what my dad calls a 'good neighborhood.'"

Joanna obviously didn't mean to think about her dad. Her whole face crumpled up, and the day that had felt safe and innocent was scrunched up in a ball and thrown away. Peijing told Biju she had a very important job: to go inside the house and bring out three cordials. Biju ran inside, and Peijing sat Joanna down on the bench out on the veranda.

"I really did want you to come over. But at the same time, I was also ashamed of the small and dirty house I lived in with Dad," said Joanna.

"You don't have to be," said Peijing. "Remember when you said you shouldn't care about what other people think because they will judge you anyway? My Ah Ma's ancestral home in Malaysia is a wooden hut that doesn't even have running water. Not even in the toilet. But I don't care."

"My dad says we should hate the horrible people that come from overseas and take all the good houses and the nice things from us. I tried to believe the same thing too. Until I realized that he was the horrible person."

Peijing put her hand over Joanna's hand.

"Remember when you also said you are not your father? You are the jade rabbit. You're braver than he could ever be."

They both looked up at the faint outline of the moon, visible in the blue sky. And Peijing realized the sky wasn't so scary after all; it was just big because it was full of endless opportunities. Peijing closed her eyes and breathed out, and the remainder of that safe and innocent day became unscrunched and smoothed out by her hands. It wasn't completely flat and perfect anymore, but it didn't matter.

"I think you're the jade rabbit, too," said Joanna. "Maybe we all are, a little bit."

Biju came crashing backward through the front screen door, holding on to three mugs at the same time. She handed one proudly to Joanna, who took a long slurp and then smiled. Peijing was embarrassed that her family owned no glasses—they drank everything from mugs, even water—but she tried not to mind because Joanna didn't seem to mind. Peijing took a sip and scrunched up her face. She did mind that Biju had made it far too sweet!

"Let's go inside," said Pejing.

Joanna nodded. She left her bicycle on the veranda, unlocked. "Do I call your mum 'Mrs. Guo'?"

"No, you call her Aunty."

"Hello . . . Aunty," said Joanna, coming face-to-face with Ma Ma again.

Ma Ma looked at Joanna in surprise. Her mouth opened to say something, then it closed again. At least Ma Ma did not look angry, thought Peijing. Not like that day so long ago at the airport, back on the other side, when Biju brought over a friend and that friend called Ma Ma by her first name.

Peijing burst out laughing and couldn't stop.

"Did I say something wrong?" asked Joanna, confused.

"No, you're fine!" replied Peijing. "Come and sit down!"

Ma Ma watched the three of them for a while, then she went over to the chest freezer to take out a packet of shumai. She put the little dumplings into the microwave to steam.

From its secret place, Peijing and Biju brought out the Little World, and Joanna sat between them, amazement on her face as it was unpacked in full on the dining table. She kept saying, "Wow," and that both of them must come and visit her and Granny, 'cos Granny was an artist and she would love to see the Little World.

Peijing felt all these sad emotions building up inside of her, getting mixed up with the fond feelings she had about the Little World, and she didn't want that. She didn't want to look at the Little World each night and think of Joanna.

"What are you having for dinner?" Joanna asked. "Can I please stay?"

"Can she stay?" Peijing asked Ma Ma excitedly, as she placed the plate of shumai on the table.

Ma Ma nodded. She looked happy that it was her night to cook, since even after a second and third round of Spamghetti night she had still not become a fan.

Peijing and Biju both cheered. But then Peijing remembered something.

Oh, no. They were having Leftover Stew.

With the exception of the nights when Ba Ba was cooking one of his wonderful inventions, Ma Ma would save all the meat and vegetable leftovers from dinner, and on the fifth day—which happened to be today—she would boil it all together with broth and pickled mustard greens. A traditional recipe handed down from Ah Ma.

Peijing was mortified. You never knew what you were going to get each time. Of all the nights that they had respectable dinners with proper dishes or even Spamghetti or spicy spaghetti night, Joanna had to come on the night they ate slop soup!

While Joanna was on the phone with her granny, Peijing went to the stove and lifted the lid of the big stockpot. The tangy smell of the pickled mustard greens escaped, and Peijing quickly shut the lid. There was no way Joanna was going to eat that!

As the clock ticked closer to dinnertime, Ah Ma came in from the living room, where she had been sitting listlessly in front of the TV, to sit at the table. Ba

Ba made loud and cheerful conversation with Joanna and wanted to know all about Australian life. Peijing looked out the dining room window into the darkening sky.

The moon was still a thin smiling crescent. Where did the jade rabbit go when the moon was gone? If he was still there and looked down at her through the same window, would he think how perfect and warm her family looked from a distance, even though it was a little broken up close? Would the jade rabbit, so far away, really understand anyway? All sacrifices were different.

Joanna watched intently as Ma Ma ladled Leftover Stew over her bowl of white steamed rice. Fish balls, carrot, baby corn spears, and a chicken drumstick tumbled out with the broth, along with the pungent-smelling mustard greens. A spoon and a fork were set out for her, but Joanna noticed that everyone else had chopsticks, so she asked for chopsticks too.

The family watched as Joanna performed strange acts of baton twirling with them. She finished one bowl and then asked for another. Peijing was ravenous too, and she found herself taking care as she ate her portion, surprised and then thankful when she found a whole steamed wonton hidden in the middle.

Leftover Stew had always been, well, Leftover Stew. But seeing how much Joanna liked it made her think of it in a new light. It was a reminder of what was good in life, of things being rescued and repurposed and of things that didn't seem compatible coming together and tasting all right. She couldn't help but be fond of Leftover Stew.

Ba Ba retold a story about his first ever day at work in Australia that had an unusual and funny twist. Ma Ma smiled and said that when she started work on Saturday she hoped she'd come home with an even funnier story to tell. That spark in Ma Ma's eyes, that competitive streak that hadn't been seen since the night of the mooncake, had come back. Ah Ma remembered with surprise that Leftover Stew was her recipe, and Biju showed Joanna how to lever the chopsticks up and down, up and down.

"You are so lucky," Joanna whispered to Peijing quietly.

Peijing looked at Ma Ma, Ba Ba, Biju, and Ah Ma in turn, and she knew that, despite what they were not, she loved them for what they were.

"The nian got such a big fright it didn't have the chance to eat even one child," said Biju. "It ran back up to the mountains and was never seen again.

"But every year the villagers make sure they wear red and make lots of noise in case it comes back. That was how Lunar New Year started."

"What ever happened to the nian?" asked Peijing, who cared about everything and everyone.

"It became vegetarian," replied Biju, and she drew a peony.

CHAPTER TWENTY-EIGHT

When it was time for Joanna to go, Peijing hoped that Ma Ma no longer thought that all the people in Australia were strange and hostile. Peijing reminded herself to be patient. They were all changing and growing at their own rates, like different seeds ready for the sun at different times. Biju fell asleep on the couch, tired out by the amount of life inside of her.

It was hard standing out on the veranda waiting for Joanna's granny to arrive. Peijing drew into herself and folded her arms. She was never going to get close to another friend like this again. Everything always ended. Everyone always left. It seemed like a better idea to stay on the safe side of life and not get too close to anything or anyone.

Peijing snuck a look at Joanna under the bare

lightbulb swirling with moths. She noticed how differently they held themselves. Peijing had her hands clasped tightly in front of her, shoulders hunched, trying to make herself as small as she could so that the world might pass her by and leave her unharmed. Joanna stood next to her with her eyes closed and her head back, her arms by her side. As Peijing watched her, Joanna lifted her arms out and upward. Joanna was unafraid.

A low hum came from her.

"What are you doing?" asked Peijing.

"I'm just asking for all the good things in the cosmos to come to me," said Joanna, her eyes still shut.

"What is the cosmos?" asked Peijing.

"The cosmos is everything. It is all the planets and all the worlds and all the stars and all of us at the same time. The Little World. Your family. My granny. You and me. Everything of everything."

How on earth could everything be everything?

Joanna opened her eyes. "Come with me," she said and grabbed Peijing by the hand. Together they ran down to the middle of the driveway.

"Go on, close your eyes."

Peijing looked skeptically at Joanna and shivered in the dark, but Joanna already had her own eyes closed and her arms out. Maybe she had already become part of the cosmos.

Closing her own eyes and stretching her arms outward, Peijing tried to see what Joanna was seeing. But all Peijing could see were all things that were wrong, all the things that had no answers that made her eyes flutter uncomfortably behind her lids.

She was going to tell Joanna it was no use when she noticed something. It was the beating of her heart, right there in the dark. She could feel it. And as she listened carefully with all her being, she noticed that the gulps of air she was desperately pulling into her lungs slowed.

She felt herself inhale and exhale as if she had a purpose. It was then that Peijing discovered that she was breathing.

Not desperately as if to keep from drowning, not trying to cool the flames of her heart constantly on fire, but breathing as if she was actually living. The slower and more deeply she breathed, the more she believed she was actually disappearing into the night.

As if her body was knitted from the same fabric that everything that surrounded her was made from. She became really small, like a beating pulse, and then felt really big, like an entire galaxy, all at the same time.

She wasn't sure if her feet were touching the ground anymore. She counted slowly down from her favorite number.

Five.

Four.

Three.

Two.

One.

She felt herself float all the way to the moon. There she saw what she thought were unfortunate pockmarks were beautiful seabeds. The Sea of Knowledge. Sea of Crises. Sea of Clouds. She let go of the snakes that had troubled her so and left them in the Serpent Sea. There on the surface she could finally see the jade rabbit—his ears, his body, and his long hind feet. She could also see the pestle in front of him for making that potion of immortality.

I made a sacrifice a long time ago, said the jade rabbit. My friend the monkey offered a starving man fruits from a tree, the otter a fish from the river, and the jackal hunted a lizard. I had nothing to offer, so I jumped upon the fire to offer myself. The starving man revealed himself to be the moon goddess, looking for a friend, and she took my skin to the moon so that all could see my sacrifice.

But what about my family? Peijing said sadly. *Where*

is there room for me? I don't want to be so far away from them out here in space.

The cosmos showed Peijing a mooncake cut into four pieces.

She saw Ba Ba, Ma Ma, Ah Ma, and Biju.

The pieces parted from one another, and revealed inside was the whole of the moon, suspended like a golden preserved yolk.

You are the heart of your family, said the cosmos. *Be the moon.*

The wobbly and slightly out-of-tune strains of "Happy Birthday" floated through the night. Peijing opened her eyes to see a group of children carrying a cake all lit up with sparklers in the park across the road.

Peijing grabbed Joanna's hand, and her friend's eyes flickered open. She looked at the scene in front of them and smiled.

"The cosmos!" she declared.

The cake was placed onto a picnic blanket, and the sparklers were plucked off the top. They went racing off into the night like burning stars, carried by invisible bodies. A memory stirred in Peijing's mind, as if the cosmos was today and yesterday and all the days at once.

Peijing and Joanna watched the lights dancing in

the night until they were joined by two comets with long yellow tails. It was the headlights of a car pulling into the driveway; it was Joanna's granny.

Excitedly, Joanna ran toward the car, forgetting that she was still joined to Peijing. Peijing was pulled unexpectedly forward, down the slope, so everything rushed at the same time into her stomach. But for once it was not a knotty or nervous feeling. It felt exhilarating, as if she were hurtling through space to somewhere unknown and anything in the future could be possible. The snakes were swimming elsewhere in the Serpent Sea.

"Granny!" exclaimed Joanna.

Peijing looked through the driver's window to see a kind-looking woman sitting there. She had blue hair, and so many beads circled around her neck that when she moved, they all clicked together as if they were typing out a story.

That's when Peijing hesitated to let go. If she held on to Joanna's hand forever, they could stay in this perfect moment.

Joanna stood there, not tearing away, as if she knew it had to be Peijing's decision.

Peijing squeezed their hands even tighter together. Then she let go.

Joanna ran to the other side of the car and jumped into the passenger's seat.

She had to let Joanna go. Joanna was going to be happy with her new family and her new school and her new life. Peijing hoped that Joanna would not put her in a box along with her bad old life and forget about her.

"The cosmos!" shouted Joanna from the car. "Remember the cosmos! Time does not exist in the cosmos!"

"I'll see you—in the cosmos!" Peijing shouted back as the car drove away. An arm stuck itself out of the rolled-down window and waved.

Peijing ran back indoors to find Biju still snoozing on the couch.

"I have a story," said Biju, halfway between asleep and awake, still made of stardust.

Peijing bundled her sister up in her arms. She carried the heavy, complaining body to the bedroom, Biju's arms around her neck, and she felt the wonder of knowing this exact moment had happened before and would in the future happen again, mirror reflections forevermore. That they would be two sisters, then two grown-ups, then two old women who would always carry each other. That they were a storyteller and an artist, a folk story that was just beginning to be told and illustrated in the cosmos. That they were twin stars. One fiery orange and one pale and white. One slightly bigger than the other. Joined by an invisible force. Dancing together.

"Tell me the story," said Peijing.

"The dragon should have been the first to cross that finish line, but she didn't because she stopped to make it rain on a dried-up rice paddy and she stopped to put out a village on fire. The jade emperor wanted to know why she came fourth. Do you know why?"

"Why?" asked Peijing.

"She said that on her way over the river, she saw a little rabbit clinging onto a log for dear life, so she gave it a gentle blow. So that the rabbit could sail over to the other side like he was on a surfboard. The dragon should have come third, you know," said Biju. "You don't get prizes in real life for coming in fourth."

Peijing thought about this carefully. It was true, there wasn't usually a medal for fourth prize. But to be honest, she would much prefer to run her own race in life, at her own pace. Just to have an opportunity was enough.

CHAPTER TWENTY-NINE

The family sat together at the table for breakfast, a regular occurrence now. Ba Ba made fried hash browns and fried slices of Spam. Ma Ma nodded and agreed the Spam tasted better this way and ate two slices. Peijing cut the food into nice small pieces for Ah Ma and reminded her to chew carefully.

The Little World was now no longer a secret, but but sat on the table openly. The red barn. A forest. An ocean. Neither Peijing nor Biju could tell when this actually happened. It was so gradual, like the shifting and melting of a giant iceberg. For some reason Biju seemed half-hearted, distracted. She kept looking out the window longingly.

"What about all the alpacas?" asked Peijing.

"I think I'm over alpacas." Biju sighed.

"I thought you loved alpacas?"

"I do," replied Biju, "but . . ."

"That's okay," said Peijing quickly. "You can put it away now."

Biju seemed relieved as she swept everything back into the box. Peijing watched her with strange emotions. She knew that Biju was going to grow out of their secret world one day, but she never expected Biju to grow out of it before she did.

But just recently, Ba Ba had purchased her a beautiful art folio filled with large high-quality sheets of paper. Peijing had been shy at first, afraid to touch the gift. It looked too shiny, too extravagant, too much. She didn't do real art at home, trying to confine it to just another subject she did at school. But, unable to resist, she flung the folio open. In time she found herself experimenting with drawing star charts and planets, things of a more sophisticated and expansive nature. Maybe she was slowly outgrowing the Little World too.

And just like that, like the shifting tectonic plates and the natural movement of the continents of planet earth, Peijing and Biju would find themselves drifting away from the Little World so slowly that one day, when they stopped playing with it, they wouldn't even pause to notice. And it was for the best as, unlike a sudden extinction, the final silent extinguishing of a star once all life had ceased upon it was a gentle and fitting good-bye.

"Peijing and Biju, there is something I need to tell you," said Ba Ba.

"Yes?" they both said at the same time.

"I want you to know something important. We're going to visit a special home this weekend."

Peijing did not say anything.

"You understand that Ah Ma has not been herself for a long time and that it is getting hard for us to look after her."

"I understand," said Peijing, and it came out of her mouth as just words with no meaning.

This is the moment where we draw together, Peijing wanted to shout. *Can't you see we are so close? We've almost made it. We should stay close to one another.*

"It's for the best," Ba Ba said. "Ah Ma will go and live at the Sea of Tranquility Retirement Home, where she will get the best of care."

From the silhouette of the moon, Peijing was sure she could hear the sound of the rabbit drumming his feet, like a call to action. She was glad that she was getting used to the food, her school, the people, and everything else that was new in Australia, but she decided that she wanted to keep some of the old things too.

Like honor. And mooncakes, once she figured out how to get them here. And looking after your family once they got old.

The drumming of rabbit feet intensified.

As they all walked across the park together to school with Ba Ba, Peijing was no longer scared at how big the world was. If only she could, through her own will, keep her little family tight-knit and all together in it. Biju said she changed her mind about drama and was going to become a champion long-distance runner instead, taking off like a rocket.

Aerobics class did not shine like it did on any other day. Peijing knew the song playing—it was in fact her favorite because it mentioned an eye belonging to a tiger and it always made her think of the Little World. But today Peijing couldn't move like the world wasn't watching. She missed all the crucial transitions, and she couldn't seem to make her body do what it was supposed to.

Back in class, Miss Lena noticed that Peijing was struggling and beckoned her to come over. Peijing went up to the teacher's desk and stood there politely.

"Is today a little hard?" asked Miss Lena.

Peijing nodded her head. She may have discovered a

small key to the universe, but big things that happened in her world, like losing a best friend, were still hard.

"I have some good news for you. I was going to save it for the end of the day, but I thought you might like to hear it now."

Peijing nodded again.

"Do you remember in art class when you made a poster for the Summerlake Surf Lifesaving Club? To stop people diving into unsafe waters?"

Peijing nodded eagerly, her heart thumping.

"Well, the good news is that your entry has made it to the short list of six posters. You got chosen out of all the other schools around here. Well done, Peijing, you're a great artist!"

Peijing had never been called an artist before.

"Even better, Joanna also made the short list. Is that a bit of a smile I see on your face? I hope so." Miss Lena handed Peijing a slip of paper with an address and a time on it.

"The presentation is this weekend. Shall I see you there? Good luck, Peijing. I really mean it."

"Thank you," said Peijing, and the words came out very soft and small, but clear.

There was no denying it. Peijing missed Joanna terribly as she sat by herself in the magic tree. It was one thing to be there side by side with someone who had problems too. It was another thing to sit alone with your own.

"Are we going to get into trouble?" came the voice out of nowhere.

Peijing pressed herself against the wall of the tree and froze.

"Isn't this considered off school grounds? Or is it right on the borderline?"

Gem's face popped through the entrance, and then the rest of her body followed. She entered without being asked and sat down cross-legged.

"How did you know I was here?"

"I followed you," replied Gem. "In fact, I've always wondered where you and Joanna used to go. I wish you would have asked me, maybe even just the once."

Peijing never thought Gem wanted to come to the magic tree too. She seemed so mature, like she would actually laugh at the idea of magic. In fact, Peijing never thought about Gem at all. But now that the girl was here, she couldn't ask her to leave because she looked right at home.

"What do you know about the Sea of Tranquility Retirement Home?" Peijing blurted out.

"You are a bit young for a retirement village, don't

you think?" said Gem. When Peijing did not reply, she added, "That's a joke, by the way."

"Is it . . . like a hospital?" asked Peijing. She had images in her head of a white room run by nurses. It was further compounded by the image from a story-book where two grandfathers and two grandmothers all shared a bed together, and Peijing had in her head a miserable picture of Ah Ma sleeping head to toe with other people's grandparents.

"Grandma Snowshoe lives at the Sea of Tranquility Retirement Home," said Gem. "It's more like a big house. Grandma has her own room, which we've decorated with her personal things. All the residents eat at the same table, and then they can hang out in this big living room together. They have bingo, and choirs that come and sing to them, and they all get to go on excursions on the bus."

Peijing listened carefully. It would be nice for Ah Ma to learn to play bingo and listen to a choir sing and go on excursions on a bus. All she did at home was sit in front of the TV or sit outside on the con-crete patio out the back and look at nothing.

"Now, what have you got for lunch?" Gem pro-duced a sandwich wrapped in cling film. "I've got Vegemite and margarine. Again. But you can have half. Wanna swap?"

Moving the bento box in front of her because she had been too sad to eat, Peijing opened the lid and showed Gem the fried rice, omelette, and stir-fried *kai lan*.

"I don't want the green veggie thing, but I'll have the rest," said Gem.

Peijing narrowed one of her eyes at the girl. She was a bit different from Joanna. But she gave the girl half of her fried rice and omelette.

"I might see you at the Sea of Tranquility Retirement Home on the weekend, then?" said Gem, talking with her mouth open.

"I'll look out for you," replied Peijing. She bit into the Vegemite and margarine sandwich. It was the very worst thing she had ever tasted, and her eyes watered. Gem laughed, and, despite it all, Peijing ended up laughing too.

CHAPTER THIRTY

Peijing thought she would be wearing her school uniform. Then it dawned on her that the ceremony was on a Saturday. In the mirror attached to her dresser, Peijing stared at the pink Garfield T-shirt and her denim shorts. She wondered if she looked immature, but she decided that she really liked the cartoon, so the shirt was going to stay.

Peijing bunched her hair to one side of her head, but she still looked nothing like the girls in the teen magazines. She dropped it back upon her shoulder, and this time she laughed at herself in the mirror. It didn't seem like such a big deal anymore.

Biju was dressing herself in the bathroom. Lately, she had decided she was too shy to stand around in her underwear with her sister in the room. Peijing thought it was possibly a passing stage, that Biju would go back to being an exhibitionist the next week. Or maybe not.

Peijing did know that, one day, Biju would move permanently out of their shared bedroom and claim the junk room next door as her own. This made her sentimental and sad, but she also knew that it was natural and that they were both growing up.

Biju came barreling into the bedroom that instant, and Peijing just had to smile. Her sister was also wearing a Garfield T-shirt and a pair of denim shorts. Peijing fell backward on her bed laughing.

"What's so funny?" Biju pouted and put her hands on her hips.

"Look at us," said Peijing. The both of them stood side by side and examined themselves in the mirror.

It seemed so long ago when Ma Ma had put the both of them in the blue satin dresses to board the airplane to Australia. It even seemed like a long time ago when they had worn the same dresses to Gem's birthday party. Now, having the choice to dress themselves for a special occasion, they found themselves still, ironically, making the identical choice.

"Do you want me to get changed?" asked Biju in a solemn voice.

"Are you embarrassed you are dressed the same as me?" said Peijing. She smiled, sure that the conversation was supposed to be the other way around.

"No," said Biju.

"In that case, I'm okay with it if you are."

Both of them smiled into the mirror. For all the things that changed, Peijing found it comforting that some things stayed the same.

A further surprise awaited them in the living room. Ba Ba was wearing the Father's Day tie Peijing had once made him at school. He hadn't thrown it out after all. In fact, he had brought it all the way to Australia, and now it hung in front of him, the color combination terrible and the sewing crooked, but Ba Ba grinned like a winner.

Peijing had been nervous when she had told Ba Ba about the prize ceremony. Something inside of her still clung onto the memory of the Mother Bear mask all stained on the inside with tears, still believed he wouldn't want to come and watch.

But the same Ba Ba who had enjoyed Biju's school play, who walked with them to school in the mornings even though he was now back at work, who lived life a little slower now, said he would love to come. That the whole family was going to come. Biju, Ah Ma, and even Ma Ma, too.

Ba Ba had made a big deal of the whole thing over dinner, and Peijing remembered the times when he never talked at the table. She marveled at the ability of people who she thought she knew so much about to change and to become their own person. Even though Peijing was quite certain she wasn't going to win, there was a humble sense of optimism buzzing throughout the whole family.

It was broken only by the fact that before they went to the prize ceremony, they had an appointment to visit the Sea of Tranquility Retirement Home. The Guo family now had their fair share of cracks, but they still held on.

Ma Ma and Ah Ma sat quietly in the back seat with Biju in the middle, while Peijing sat up front as the guest of honor. The air-conditioning was broken, even though the car was new, so all four windows were wound all the way down. The white car rattled and whistled along the highway like a rice cooker. Peijing closed her eyes against the wind, and she dared it to rip her emotions from her.

The Sea of Tranquility Retirement Home was a group of redbrick houses that were connected together by pathways and gardens filled with tea roses and banksias in bloom. It was certainly tranquil, but there was no sea there, not even a little one. Peijing felt better that it looked nothing like a hospital, that the foyer they walked into looked more like a normal house.

"Hi, Peijing," said Gem. She was standing at the front counter with an old lady in a wheelchair. "Oh, hello, Biju, we meet again."

Biju grinned and sidled up to Gem.

"Hi," said Peijing. She shuffled awkwardly, overwhelmed at the possibility of introductions.

"Hey, congratulations on being a finalist in the Look Before You Dive competition. I hope you win," said Gem, filling out the book on the desk. "We're taking Grandma to the beach. Waiting for Dad to bring the van. See you, I guess?"

"See you," replied Peijing firmly. Gem and Grandma Snowshoe disappeared quickly out the front door. Now gone, she wished Gem would have stayed longer and reassured her that the Sea of Tranquility Retirement Home was the right place for Ah Ma to live.

"Ah, the Guo Family," said a pleasant-looking woman who did not quite pronounce their name right.

"What do you think?" whispered Peijing to Ah Ma as the tour took them inside a bedroom that was empty except for a bed.

"It's very nice," replied Ah Ma.

The lady said the room had just become available and that this would be Ah Ma's room if she came to stay. Nobody asked what had happened to the person who lived in the room before.

"What about this?" whispered Peijing as they looked into a big room with lots of tables in which all the residents were seated. A person at the front was winding the handle of a wire cage and spinning all these colored balls inside. A ball dropped out the bottom, and the person called out, "B eleven!" An old gentleman stood up excitedly on his frail legs and shouted, "Bingo!"

"It's very nice," replied Ah Ma. The man who'd called out "Bingo" was given a block of chocolate as a prize, and the game continued. A group of older ladies noticed Biju and tried to call her over like a puppy, but Biju hid behind Ba Ba.

Peijing looked discreetly over Ba Ba's shoulder and noted that the time on his watch was creeping close to the time of the awards ceremony. She grew anxious that the tour was taking too long and that they would be late, but she took a deep breath and made herself small, put the bigger importance of her family and Ah Ma first.

In the kitchen, two cooks were busy preparing lunch. Ma Ma inspected it silently with a downturned mouth. Everything was presented on the same seg-mented plate, regardless of whether it was solid food or green, orange, and white pureed blobs instead. It was all Western foods. Peijing was worried that Ah Ma wouldn't be able to eat it, but then she remem-bered how Ah Ma loved Spamghetti. She even loved Ba Ba's latest invention: clamghetti.

"Is this okay?" whispered Peijing.

"It's very nice," said Ah Ma, smiling.

The last part of the tour was of the gardens out-side. The lady was very keen to point out how much outdoor space there was and the different benches to sit on.

"So, Ah Ma, do you think you can live here?" asked Ba Ba cheerfully.

"No," said Ah Ma.

"But you said it was nice," said Peijing, nudging her. "I am sure you will like it here."

The realization that everyone was planning to abandon her at this strange place suddenly dawned on Ah Ma.

"No!" she yelled. "I want to go home! I belong with my husband and my children! My youngest is still a baby and hasn't even learned how to crawl yet. Help me, Jiazeng!"

Everyone was horrified. Jiazeng was Ah Gong's

337

name, and he had gone to the land of the ghosts a long time ago.

Ma Ma tried to shush Ah Ma, but she refused to be shushed. Ba Ba apologized to the lady giving the tour, who gave him a very understanding face. He promised that after Ah Ma calmed down they were going back inside to sign some forms. Peijing felt like her head was about to explode.

The scene was interrupted by a loud, piercing scream.

Everyone stopped and looked down at Biju.

"Stop!" she yelled loudly. "You can't treat Ah Ma like this!"

"Help me," repeated Ah Ma in a daze.

Biju took Ah Ma by the hand.

"Run!" she ordered Ah Ma, and both of them started running. Biju trying to sprint on ahead, Ah Ma trying her best on her old and aching knees. Ba Ba, Ma Ma, Peijing, and the lady giving them the tour stared dumbfounded, unsure of what to do.

Peijing was the first to snap out of it. She started chasing them.

"Quick, this way!" shouted Biju, and that was when Peijing realized she wasn't chasing them down, she was joining them.

CHAPTER THIRTY-ONE

Around the corner of one of the redbrick houses they hurried, an awkward team where all three members ran in completely different styles, holding hands.

Onto the Sea of Tranquility Retirement Home parking lot they spilled. In front of them was the Guo family car.

"We're making an escape," said Biju firmly. The only problem Peijing could see wrong with this wonderful getaway plan was that none of them could drive.

"Drats. Foiled," said Biju, and they all slowed down. But Biju was still holding on and so was Peijing, Ah Ma suspended between them.

A horn beeped in welcome, and they turned their heads.

"Not necessarily!" said Peijing. They turned and

headed toward the white van from which Gem was waving.

"We are trying to make an escape," Biju explained to Gem.

"That's right," confirmed Peijing, who had never in her entire life ever willingly erred onto the side of wrongdoing.

But, to be honest, it felt quite exhilarating.

"Remember when you fell in alpaca poo?" said Gem, and she ruffled Biju's hair affectionately.

"Hello, cool cats and kittens," said Mr. Snowshoe from the driver's seat.

"Hi," replied Peijing, and then she clammed up. She still remembered the fear of talking to a stranger when she had to report Ah Ma missing. How awful the entire experience was. She closed her eyes and called to the cosmos. She let go of the experience, and it drifted out into space.

"Can we please have a ride?" said Peijing, opening her eyes.

"Where are you folks heading off to?" asked Mr. Snowshoe.

"The Summerlake Surf Lifesaving Club."

"Why, I can drop you right on the doorstep. We're all going to the beach. What a glorious day for it too. Let's go!"

Peijing, Biju, and Ah Ma climbed into the van and smiled at Grandma Snowshoe, who smiled back. Gem slammed the door, and the van started moving.

Through the window, Peijing watched as Ba Ba and Ma Ma, along with the lady giving the tour, came around the corner and watched in disbelief as they saw her face, along with the van, move toward the exit of the parking lot, indicate, and then drive away from the Sea of Tranquility Retirement Home.

Down the freeway the van sped. Peijing looked out the back window, and, slowly, her parents' white car came into view. The car drove up to the van and followed so closely that Peijing could see the look of displeasure on Ba Ba's face. Gem inserted herself next to Peijing.

"I see you're running away from your parents."

"Shhhh," said Peijing, turning to look at Mr. Snowshoe in the driver's seat. "Do you mind not shouting it to everyone?"

"So, why are you committing this major act of disobedience?" said Gem in a softer voice.

"Honor," replied Peijing.

The van stopped at a traffic light, and Ba Ba pulled right up to its bumper. The expression on Ba Ba's face had not changed.

"Is it such a big deal?" asked Gemma.

Peijing thought about it. About the things her parents had always taught her: respecting elders and looking after your family when they got old. About how there was a whole new set of rules to live by now that they were in Australia. Some had been harder to adjust to, but others had been easy, and they had taken to them like fish to water. She needed to let go.

But Peijing looked at Ah Ma, sitting in the comfortable seat of the van, smiling at Biju, and she could not let go. There were some things worth hanging on to. It was not about what country you lived in, or what culture you grew up in. It was what was irrevocably, globally, universally right. And a family was always worth fighting for.

The van turned off the freeway, and up a steep hill it started to go. Peijing looked back again and was slightly fearful the Guo family car was going to slide backward, but Ba Ba's face held determined and so did the wheels of the car.

The van suddenly popped up at the top and, as it started its descent downward, the ocean came into view. Peijing and Biju gasped. Even Gem, who had probably come this way many times before to take Grandma Snowshoe to the beach, sat transfixed, a serene expression on her face. Peijing could not stop the smile that she could feel twitching at the sides of her mouth. The ocean was as big as the sky. In the very best way.

The van traveled alongside the ocean, and Gem rolled down all the windows. The girls stuck their faces out to feel the breeze. From the Guo family car still following, Peijing could see a hand upon the open window, and then the side of Ma Ma's face came into view as she leaned her cheek down on her arm.

It had been a long time since the Guo family had been to the ocean. And the seaside that they had seen before, with gray-looking sand and a thin line of grayish water, was nothing like this huge expanse of blue that sucked everyone's worries toward it and threw them away upon the waves. The ocean felt like healing.

The van pulled into the Summerlake Surf Life-saving Club parking lot, and Mr. Snowshoe turned off the engine. Peijing and Biju helped Ah Ma out down the step and, giggling, they headed to the edge of the parking lot and turned to face the ocean. It was loud in their ears and fresh against their faces. Peijing felt her lungs were fit to burst.

It felt like they were standing on the very edge of the world, where everything in front of them was beyond all that they knew, but full of future adventure and within grasp as everything was part of the cosmos.

"Pearls don't lie on the shore," said Ah Ma. "If you want one, you have to dive for it."

Peijing turned to see Gem coming toward them, wheeling Grandma Snowshoe.

"It's wonderful, isn't it? Shame the day never lasts forever, but sometimes it's nice to imagine it might."

Peijing turned to see the Guo family car park itself. Their moment was also drawing to a close. A grumpy Ba Ba came out, followed by a bewildered-looking Ma Ma, who held on to his hand like a child.

"Let's go!" Peijing called loudly. She took Biju and Ah Ma's hands. "You too, Gem!"

"Am I invited?" asked Gem in surprise.

"Not if you don't hurry!"

Gem turned the wheelchair around. The whole group hurried toward the door of the clubhouse, under the astonished nose of Mr. Snowshoe, who opened the door of the van and stepped out. It looked like he had no choice but to follow them too. Behind him, Ba Ba and Ma Ma hurried close behind.

The Summerlake Surf Lifesaving Club, a wooden structure painted white, with its name on the side in a faded and peeling blue, had been looking at the ocean for more than a hundred years and would have lapsed into retirement if it had not been for volunteers who oiled the deck and mowed the patchy piece of lawn out the front. Its floorboards creaked in greeting with the unexpected weight of the new visitors.

The prize-giving was already underway when Peijing and her group stumbled in like a group of holiday-makers having taken the wrong turn. The master of ceremonies had called in this morning with a terrible illness, and the last-minute replacement was bumbling through the proceedings as best they could, even though they kept repeating things, called it a surfing competition, and told everyone where the toilets and emergency exits were twice.

The third-place winner was announced, and it was a student from a fancy school who was wearing their school uniform and blazer even though it was the weekend and a hot day. Peijing looked down, feeling unsure about her Garfield shirt.

A parent and someone from the school stood up with expensive cameras and made the embarrassed winner pose this way and that with their certificate and wrapped prize.

A hand from the back of the audience shot into the air and waved. Peijing recognized with relief that it belonged to Miss Lena and hurried over. As she reached her teacher, an excitement started to build inside of her. Biju, Ah Ma, Gem, Grandma Snowshoe, and Mr. Snowshoe followed, along with Ba Ba and Ma Ma, who, finding themselves in a public situation, perhaps thought it was not the right place to reprimand their daughter for running away . . . and kidnapping her younger sister and grandmother, although Peijing would like to argue that it was her who was kidnapped by them.

"Look," said Miss Lena, pointing to the front. Peijing could see her poster pinned on the display board next to Joanna's and with all the finalists from other schools.

"G'day!" boomed a voice in her ear, and Peijing turned to see Joanna sitting right behind her, along with her granny. Peijing was overjoyed to see her friend again. Maybe it was the distortion of time or her memory, but Joanna looked different. She never remembered Joanna's face having that roundness about it or that amount of life in her eyes. She looked so happy and healthy. Peijing wanted to keep staring, but she knocked knees with Gem, who insisted on sharing the same seat as her.

"Scoot over!" Gem stared at both Joanna and Peijing and then raised her fist up. "Alpaca Club!"

"What club?" said Joanna.

"Alpaca Club," said Gem, with her fist still hovering. "Forever!"

"I am part of Alpaca Club too," insisted Biju.

They all raised their fists and solemnly bumped them.

"Pejing!" said Miss Lena. "Hurry, Peijing, they just called your name!"

"What?"

CHAPTER THIRTY-TWO

Peijing stood up and waded herself past the legs of those seated in the row. It felt like she was walking in a dream. The clapping of hands was as loud as thunder and roared in time with her heartbeat. She walked up to the stage, and the master of ceremonies shook her hand and gave her a certificate and a wrapped present. She stood there staring back at the faces in the crowd, unable to see anyone.

A little group was moving and dancing at the back, and Peijing was able to focus enough to see it was the Alpaca Club. Her eyes moved slowly down the same row and located Miss Lena, Ah Ma, Grandma Snowshoe, Mr. Snowshoe, and then Ba Ba and Ma Ma. Both her parents were on their feet, and they were clapping.

The photographer got Peijing to stand next to the third-prize winner, and she felt as if her legs were going to give way. Something dislodged inside of her, and Peijing realized it was both the fear of cauliflower hands and the fear of Extinctions. As she felt the certificate and prize in her hand, solid and real, she knew that they reflected something inside of her that could never be diminished or taken away.

The next thing she knew, she heard Joanna's name being called, followed by the loud public holler of "Alpaca Club forever!"

Joanna came all the way from the back of the audience, walked up the stage, and received her prize. Then she was suddenly next to Peijing.

"What is happening?" Joanna asked.

"You're a winner," replied Peijing.

"Oh!" said Joanna. "So are you."

They hugged each other and didn't let go.

After the photographer had taken a million photos of the three winners, they were allowed to come off the stage and mingle with the crowd to have celebratory zucchini bread and juice.

"I've got a bedroom with a beautiful bed frame made of jarrah wood. And a dressing table and all these new clothes," Joanna told Peijing breathlessly. "Will you come visit? It's only a short drive down the road and—"

"Up the hill that makes your ears pop, I know," said Peijing sadly. The exhilaration from before was just a warm glow now. The present in her hand grew heavy with her.

"I think your dad wants to talk to you," said Joanna, her eyes suddenly darting sideways. "I'll talk to you later!"

There was a firm clearing of the throat, and Peijing found herself face-to-face with Ba Ba. She didn't feel she could look him in the eyes or even think of him as "Dad," as Joanna put it. It sounded foreign, personal. Ba Ba was always only "Father" in her head.

"That was very irresponsible to run away with your sister and grandmother like that," said Ba Ba.

"I know! I was just trying to—"

"I know too," said Ba Ba. "I know that there aren't easy solutions to some things in life. I know that you were just trying to protect the family's honor, because, after all, that is what we taught you."

They both looked sadly at Ah Ma, who wasn't sad right now at all. She was talking to Ma Ma and trying to talk to Grandma Snowshoe and eating zucchini bread and sneaking some into her pockets for later.

"But I want you to know that we can still be honorable and still compromise, just like we have all come to make other compromises in Australia. And maybe that is a good thing," continued Ba Ba. "It is not good to throw yourself headfirst into something and forget your past, but it is not good to hold on to an old concept with two tight hands."

"I understand," replied Peijing, and, for once, she really honestly felt she did.

"We will do our best for Ah Ma."

Peijing nodded.

"I want you to know that I feel you're too old now for the chicken feather duster, but that doesn't mean you won't be disciplined. We will discuss it at home. But right now, I am very proud of you for winning the prize."

Peijing could feel tears in her eyes. Of course she wasn't looking forward to being disciplined, but . . . Ba Ba just told her he was proud.

"Drawing is an important skill. I should know, as I am an architect and I draw all the time. Don't stop doing it."

Peijing had never thought of her dad being an artist before, but it was true and it felt like she was suddenly seeing things from a whole new perspective. The moon always looked different when you looked at it, but it was still the same moon. There was just so much to learn and understand about the surprises and the mystery of life. She gripped the certificate more tightly. She glanced down at it, and her name, hand-drawn in curly lettering, seemed to be full of possibility.

"I've also spoken to Granny Polonaise, and she asked about you and Biju visiting sometime."

Peijing looked up at Ba Ba expectantly.

"I told her I would think about it."

Peijing suddenly found herself being propelled by a greater force, perhaps the cosmos itself, and she wrapped her arms around Ba Ba and gave him a big hug. She could feel Ba Ba stiffen in surprise, but then she felt him hug her back.

Later she would end up at Ma Ma's side and she would hug Ma Ma, too.

And Ma Ma, who enjoyed the prize ceremony and afternoon tea very much, would investigate how to enroll in evening English-speaking classes.

Peijing was able to return to Joanna with a smile and a "maybe," which was much better and more hopeful than a "no."

"We could do sleepovers, too! We can watch that space movie and eat sugared popcorn with a drop of pink food coloring!" said Joanna in excitement.

"I like space movies!" came a familiar voice. Gem stood there grinning with a slice of zucchini bread in each hand.

"So do I," said Biju, Peijing was certain Biju didn't know what a space movie was.

Peijing shook her head, but she was still smiling. One step at a time.

"Alpaca Club forever!" shouted both Gem and Biju.

Peijing hated having to part with Joanna now that she was back again, but they left each other with the promise of that future visit. The Alpaca Club reached out and touched one another's fingertips in a secret acknowledgment. Then they were separated back into their own individual cars and lives, at least for the time being.

Miss Lena drove past in her pink convertible sports car and honked loudly.

As the Guo family car traveled along the ocean drive, back toward the freeway and back toward home, Ah Ma started to tell a story about when she was a child. Biju asked her a million questions. Ma Ma leaned back into the seat with a knowing smile on her face. Ba Ba hummed along to an old song playing on the radio. The ocean breeze came in through the four open windows and soothed everyone.

And as for Peijing, still the guest of honor sitting up front, she looked proudly at the certificate in her hand. She placed it on the dashboard and looked at the gift sitting on her lap, wrapped in purple cellophane.

Surrounded by the noises of her family and alone in her own thoughts, Peijing never felt that life could be so simple and yet so intricate and delicate. At this one point in time, the Guo family was untouchable. And shining at the center of it all was Peijing.

Peijing pulled at the bow and started unwrapping the gift.

As the paper unveiled the prize in her lap, she recognized the rectangular plastic object and the attached earphones as being a personal music player. She inspected the cassette tape but did not know the artist. The photo on the front showed a young woman wearing a hat of cascading curls and a black off-the-shoulder top that was very fashionable.

Later, in the privacy of her own bedroom, away from her family, Peijing would listen to the album and then listen to it again. She would locate a larger picture of the young woman on the cassette cover and stick it up on her wall—her very first poster.

Much later, she would convince Ma Ma to buy her an off-the-shoulder top, but Ma Ma said she couldn't wear it until she was thirteen, and they came to a compromise, even though Peijing thought she was old enough.

Biju, who wanted to wear the top too, rushed to the living room to grab an old family album and pointed to all the photos of Ma Ma wearing a miniskirt at the same age. Ma Ma went red and didn't have anything to say. *Here we go again*, thought Peijing. *Adults saying one thing and doing another.* Then it occurred to her, like something magical, that this wasn't just a cultural thing. This was a thing that happened to everyone.

A growing-up thing.

Peijing could not quite believe that almost a whole year had passed. She was almost twelve now. The dressing table with the frilly skirt around it she had loved when she first arrived seemed almost too young for her now. She wondered when her parents would let her connect the princess phone next to her bed.

She never thought that she would ever get to this point in life, but before she knew it, there she was. And one day, if she wasn't careful, it would all be over, and she would wish she'd paid more attention.

So she lived in the moment, between the past and the future, between the East and the West, and found her place there.

Once upon a time lived the Guo family, who were a very Chinese family that believed in superstition and honor. They moved to Australia, where they were still very Chinese and they still believed in superstition and honor, but they were more relaxed around the edges. Sometimes they used chopsticks. Sometimes they used forks and spoons.

Every weekend, Ah Ma came back home from the Sea of Tranquility Retirement Home, and, although the guilt never went away, they tried to spend their best time with her. Ah Ma said how much she enjoyed the choir that came to sing for them and that she could even recite the words of some of the choruses; she also said she enjoyed the bus trips out, even though she had trouble recalling where it was she went.

Exactly one year later, when the moon once again became full and round, even though the rest of the family—all the aunties, uncles, and cousins—were not around, the Guo family gathered together at the family table.

Ma Ma had a surprise that she had been fussing all week about, making sure nobody peeked into a certain area of the pantry. Biju had first speculated it was a lantern, then a rabbit, and finally settled on fireworks. She could tell because she was a storyteller and always knew the ending.

It was neither of those things. Ma Ma approached the

table, and on a blue-and-white china plate sat a single moon-cake. Peijing opened her mouth in delight, and the mooncake glowed like it was illuminated from the inside.

Ma Ma said that the Asian Mart she now worked at imported them, so they were still able to celebrate Mid-Autumn Festival like they always did. She cut it into five pieces, and everyone took one except for Biju, who turned her nose up and said she still thought the preserved egg yolk inside was stinky.

"Why don't we make some with sweet bean filling for you, then, my child!" exclaimed Ah Ma, and moved toward the kitchen.

"Do you still know the recipe, Ah Ma?" Peijing asked nervously as she tagged along. Some things still made her nervous even though she wasn't scared anymore.

"I'd never forget it!" replied her grandmother as she peered into the pantry, well stocked from the Asian Mart.

"Can I learn too?" came Biju's voice.

"I thought you weren't interested," scoffed Peijing.

"Well, I am a whole year older now," replied Biju, look-ing thoughtful. "I'm not the same person I was before."

"I want to learn too," said another voice; it was Ba Ba.

"Make some room for the best mooncake maker," said Ma Ma, and she started taking bowls and utensils from the drawers.

The Guo family gathered around the breakfast bench

and made a tray of imperfect mooncakes because although Peijing and Biju weren't very good and Ba Ba even worse, it was important they played a part too. Outside, the moon hung so round and yellow it gave the huge sky above the park something to worry about.

"I feel like we have become part of a folktale," whispered Peijing to Biju. "A story that will always be passed down forever."

"I will write our story one day," said Biju. "I am interested in calisthenics and gymnastics at the moment, but I am always going to be a storyteller."

"You will make me a flattering character, won't you?" said Peijing.

"Of course," said Biju and grinned.